Books by Penelope Lively

THE ROAD TO LICHFIELD
NOTHING MISSING BUT THE SAMOVAR
TREASURES OF TIME
JUDGEMENT DAY
NEXT TO NATURE, ART
PERFECT HAPPINESS

for children

ASTERCOTE
THE WHISPERING KNIGHTS
THE WILD HUNT OF HAGWORTHY
THE DRIFTWAY
THE GHOST OF THOMAS KEMPE
THE HOUSE IN NORHAM GARDENS
GOING BACK
BOY WITHOUT A NAME
A STITCH IN TIME
FANNY'S SISTER
THE VOYAGE OF QV66
FANNY AND THE MONSTERS
FANNY AND THE BATTLE OF POTTER'S PIECE
THE REVENGE OF SAMUEL STOKES
UNINVITED GHOSTS AND OTHER STORIES

Corruption

PENELOPE LIVELY

Heinemann : London

William Heinemann Ltd
10 Upper Grosvenor Street, London W1X 9PA
LONDON   MELBOURNE   TORONTO
JOHANNESBURG   AUCKLAND

This collection first published 1984
Copyright © Penelope Lively 1980, 1981, 1982, 1984
SBN 434 42741 1

Printed and bound in Great Britain by
Biddles Limited, Guildford & King's Lynn

Contents

Corruption   1
Venice, now and then   19
Grow old along with me, the best is yet to be   29
The darkness out there   37
The pill-box   53
Customers   61
Yellow trains   71
'The ghost of a flea'   77
The art of biography   95
What the eye doesn't see   109
The emasculation of Ted Roper   127

Acknowledgements

'Venice, now and then' was first published in *Quarto*, 1980.

'The darkness out there' was first published in the Bodley Head Collection, *You Can't Keep out the Darkness*, 1980, and read on BBC radio and Australian radio.

'The ghost of a flea' was first published in *The Literary Review*, 1980.

'The art of biography' was first published in *Good Housekeeping*, 1981.

'What the eye doesn't see' was first published in *Encounter*, 1981.

'The emasculation of Ted Roper' was first published in *Encounter*, 1982.

'Corruption' was first published in *Encounter*, 1984.

'Grow old along with me, the best is yet to be' was first published in *Cosmopolitan*, 1984.

'Yellow trains' was first published in *Vogue*, 1984.

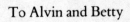

To Alvin and Betty

Corruption

The judge and his wife, driving to Aldeburgh for the weekend, carried with them in the back of the car a Wine Society carton filled with pornographic magazines. The judge, closing the hatchback, stared for a moment through the window; he reopened the door and put a copy of *The Times* on top of the pile, extinguishing the garish covers. He then got into the driving seat and picked up the road atlas. "The usual route, dear?"

"The usual route, I think. Unless we spot anything enticing on the way."

"We have plenty of time to be enticed, if we feel so inclined."

The judge, Richard Braine, was sixty-two; his wife Marjorie, a magistrate, was two years younger. The weekend ahead was their annual and cherished early summer break at the Music Festival; the pornographic magazines were the impounded consignment of an importer currently under trial and formed the contents of the judge's weekend briefcase, so to speak. "Chores?" his wife had said, and he had replied, "Chores, I'm afraid."

At lunch-time, they pulled off the main road into a carefully selected lane and found a gate-way in which to park the car. They carried the rug and picnic basket into a nearby

1

field and ate their lunch under the spacious East Anglian
sky, in a state of almost flamboyant contentment. Both had
noted how the satisfactions of life have a tendency to gain
intensity with advancing years. "The world gets more
beautiful," Marjorie had once said, "not less so. Fun is even
more fun. Music is more musical, if you see what I mean.
One hadn't reckoned with that." Now, consuming the
thoughtfully constructed sandwiches and the coffee from
the thermos, they glowed at one another amid the long
thick grass that teemed with buttercup and clover; before
them, the landscape retreated into blue distances satis-
factorily broken here and there by a line of trees, the tower
of a church or a rising contour. From time to time they
exchanged remarks of pleasure or anticipation: about the
surroundings, the weather, the meal they would eat tonight
at the little restaurant along the coast road, tomorrow
evening's concert. Richard Braine, who was a man res-
ponsive to the moment, took his wife's hand; they sat in the
sun, shirt-sleeved, and agreed conspiratorially and without
too much guilt that they were quite glad that the eldest
married daughter who sometimes accompanied them on
this trip had not this year been able to. The daughter was
loved, but would just now have been superfluous.

When they arrived at the small hotel it was early evening.
The judge carried their suitcase and the Wine Society carton
in and set them down by the reception desk. The proprietor,
bearing the carton, showed them to their usual room. As
she was unpacking, Marjorie said, "I think you should have
left that stuff in the car. Chambermaids, you know . . ."
The judge frowned. "That's a point." He tipped the contents of the box into the emptied suitcase and locked it.
"I think I'll have a bath before we go out."

He lay in the steamy cubicle, a sponge resting upon his
stomach. Marjorie, stripped to a pair of pants, came in to

2

wash. "The dear old avocado suite again. One day we must have an avocado bathroom suite at home." The judge, contemplating the rise of his belly, nodded; he was making a resolution about reduction of the flesh, a resolution which he sadly knew would be broken. He was a man who enjoyed food. His wife's flesh, in the process now of being briskly soaped and scrubbed, was firmer and less copious, as he was fully prepared to concede. He turned his head to watch her and thought for a while in a vague and melancholy way about bodies, about how we inhabit them and are dragged to the grave by them and are conditioned by them. In the course of his professional life he had frequently had occasion to reflect upon the last point: it had seemed to him, observing the faces that passed before him in courtrooms, that confronted him from docks and witness boxes, that not many of us are able to rise above physical appearance. The life of an ugly woman is different from that of a beautiful one; you cannot infer character from appearance, but you can suspect a good deal about the circumstances to which it will have given rise. Abandoning this interesting but sombre theme, he observed his wife's breasts and muscular but not unshapely thighs and the folds of skin upon her neck and remembered the first time he had seen her with no clothes on. She turned to look at him; "If you're jeering at my knickers, they're a pair of Alison's I grabbed out of the laundry basket by mistake." Alison was their youngest, unmarried daughter. "I hadn't really noticed them," said the judge politely. "I was thinking about something quite different." He smiled. "And don't leer," said his wife, flicking him with her flannel. "It's unbecoming in a man of your age." "It's a tribute to your charms, my dear," said the judge. He sat up and began to wash his neck, thinking still about that first time; they had both been embarrassed. Embarrassment had been a part of the pleasure, he reflected. How odd, and interesting.

3

It was still daylight when they drove to the restaurant, a violet summer twilight in which birds sang with jungle stridency. Marjorie, getting out of the car, said, "That veal and mushroom in cream sauce thing for me, I think. A small salad for you, without dressing."

"No way," said the judge.

"I admire your command of contemporary speech." She went ahead into the restaurant, inspecting the room with bright, observant eyes. When they were sitting at the table she whispered, "There's that same woman we met last year. Remember? The classy type who kept putting you right about Britten".

The judge, cautiously, turned his head. "So it is. Keep a low profile."

"Will do, squire," said Marjorie, applying herself to the menu. "Fifteen all?" she added, "Right?"

"Right," said her husband.

Their acquaintance, leaving before them, stopped to exchange greetings. The judge, mildly resenting the interruption to his meal, left the work to Marjorie. The woman, turning to go, said. "So nice to see you again. And have a lovely break from juries and things." She gleamed upon the judge.

He watched her retreating silk-clad back. "Rather a gushing creature. How the hell does she know what I do?"

"Chatting up the hotel people, I don't doubt. It gives you cachet, you note, your job. Me, on the other hand, she considers a drab little woman. I could see her wondering how I came by you."

"Shall we enlighten her? Sheer unbridled lust . . ."

"Talking of which," said Marjorie, "Just how unprincipled would it be to finish off with some of that cheesecake?"

Back at the hotel, they climbed into bed in a state of

4

enjoyable repletion. The judge put on his spectacles and reached out for the suitcase. "You're not going to start going through that stuff *now* . . ." said Marjorie. "At least have one whole day off work."

"You're right," he said. "Tomorrow will do. I'll have that Barbara Pym novel instead."

The judge, waking early the next morning, lay thinking about the current trial. He thought, in fact, not about obscenity or pornography but about the profit motive. He did not, he realised, understand the profit motive; he did not understand it in the same way in which he did not understand what induced people to be cruel. He had never coveted the possessions of others or wished himself richer than he was. He held no stocks or shares; Marjorie, once, had been left a small capital sum by an aunt; neither he nor she had ever been able to take the slightest interest in the financial health of her investments. Indeed, both had now forgotten what exactly the money was in. All this, he realised, was the position of a man with a substantial earned income; were he not paid what he was he might well feel otherwise. But he had not, in fact, felt very much otherwise as an impecunious young barrister. And importers of pornography tend, he understood, to be in an upper income bracket. No – the obstacle, the barrier requiring that leap of the imagination, was this extra dimension of need in some men that sought to turn money into yet more money, that required wealth for wealth's sake, the spawning of figures. The judge himself enjoyed growing vegetables; he considered, now, the satisfaction he got from harvesting a good crop of french beans and tried to translate this into a manifestation of the profit motive. The analogy did not quite seem to work.

The profit motive in itself, of course, is innocuous enough. Indeed, without it societies would founder. This was not the point that was bothering the judge; he was interested in those gulfs of inclination that divide person from person. As a young man he had wondered if this restriction makes us incapable of passing judgement on our fellows, but had come to realise at last that it does not. He remembered being involved in an impassioned argument about apartheid with another law student, an Afrikaner; "You cannot make pronouncements on our policies," the man had said, "when you have never been to our country. You cannot understand the situation." Richard Braine had known, with the accuracy of a physical response, that the man was wrong. Not misguided; simply wrong. A murderer is doing wrong, whatever the circumstances that drive him to his crime.

The profit motive is not wrong; the circumstances of its application may well be. The judge – with a certain irritation – found himself recalling the features of the importer of pornography: a nondescript, bespectacled man memorable only for a pair of rather bushy eyebrows and a habit of pulling an ear-lobe when under cross-examination. He pushed the fellow from his mind, determinedly, and got out of bed. Outside the window, strands of neatly corrugated cloud coasted in a milky-blue sky; it looked as though it would be a nice day.

The Braines spent the morning at Minsmere bird sanctuary; in the afternoon they went for a walk. The evening found them, scoured by fresh air and slightly somnolent, listening to Mozart, Bartok and Mendelssohn. The judge, who had never played an instrument and regarded himself as relatively unmusical, nevertheless responded to music with considerable intensity. It aroused him in various ways; in such different ways, indeed, that, being a thorough and methodical man, he often felt bemused, caught up by the onward rush of events before he had time to sort them out. Stop, he wanted to say to the surging orchestra, just let me have a think about that bit . . . But already he would have been swept onwards, into other moods, other themes, other passions. Marjorie, who played the piano in an unspectacular but competent way, had often suggested that the problem might be solved at least in part if he learned to read music.

She was no doubt right, he thought, wrestling now with a tortuous passage. When I retire; just the thing for a man reduced to inactivity. The judge did not look forward to retirement. But a few moments of inattention had been fatal – now the music had got away from him entirely, as though he had turned over two pages of a book. Frowning, he concentrated on the conductor.

Standing at the bar in the interval, he found himself beside their acquaintance from the restaurant, also waiting to order a drink. Gallantry or even basic good manners required that he intervene. "Oh," she said. "How terribly sweet of you. A gin and tonic would be gorgeous." With resignation, he led her back to where Marjorie awaited him.

"Your husband was so sweet and insistent – I'm all on my own this evening, my sister had a splitting headache and decided not to come." She was a tall woman in her early fifties, too youthfully packaged in a flounced skirt and high-heeled boots, her manner towards the judge both sycophantic and faintly roguish. "I was reading about you in *The Times* last month, some case about people had up for embezzling, of course I didn't understand most of it, all terribly technical, but I said to Laura. I *know* him, we had such a lovely talk about Britten at the Festival."

"Ah," said the judge, studying his programme: the Tippett next.

"I'm Moira Lukes, by the way – if you're anything like me names just *evaporate*, but of course I remembered yours from seeing it in the paper." She turned to Marjorie, "Aren't

7

you loving the concert?"; patronage discreetly flowed, the patronage of a woman with a sexual history towards one who probably had not, of a lavishly clad woman towards a dowdy one. The judge's antennae slightly quivered, though he was not himself sure why. Marjorie blandly agreed that the concert was superb. "Excuse me," she said. "I'm going to make a dash to the loo while there's time."

The judge and Moira Lukes, left alone, made private adjustments to each other's company: the judge cleared his throat and commented on the architecture of the concert hall; Moira moved a fraction closer to him and altered the pitch of her voice, probably without being aware that she did either. "You must lead such a fascinating life," she said. "I mean, you must come across such extraordinary people. Dickensian types. I don't think I've ever set eyes on a criminal."

The judge thought again of the importer of pornography. "Most of them are rather mundane, when it comes to the point."

"But you must get to know so much about people." She was looking very directly at him, with large eyes; a handsome woman, the judge conceded, rather a knock-out as a girl, no doubt. He agreed that yes, one did get a few insights into the ways in which people carry on.

"Fascinating," said Moira Lukes again. "I expect you have the most marvellous stories to tell. I envy your wife no end." The large eyes creased humorously at the corners; a practised device, though the judge did not recognise this. "In fact I think she's a lucky woman – I still remember that interesting chat you and I had last year." And she laid on his arm a hand, which was almost instantly removed – come and gone as briefly as though a bird had alighted for a fleeting second. The judge, startled in several ways, tried to recall this chat: something about when *Peter Grimes* was first

8

performed, or was it *The Turn of the Screw*? The interest of it, now, escaped him. He cast a quick glance across the foyer in search of Marjorie, who seemed to be taking an awfully long time. Moira Lukes was talking now about the area of Sussex in which she lived. Do, she was saying, look in and have lunch, both of you, if you're ever in that part of the world. The judge murmured that yes, of course if ever they were . . . He noticed the rings on her hand and wondered vaguely what had become of Mr Lukes; somehow one knew that he was no longer around, one way or the other.

"The only time," she said, "I've ever personally had anything to do with the law was over my rather wretched divorce." The judge took a swig of his drink. "And then actually the lawyer was most awfully sweet, in fact he kept my head above water through it all." She sighed, a whiff of a sigh, almost imperceptible; thereby, she implied most delicately, hung a tale. "So I've got rather a soft spot for legal people."

"Good," said the judge heartily. "I'm glad to hear you've been well treated by the profession."

"Oh, *very* well treated."

No sign of Marjorie, still. Actually, the judge was thinking, this Moira Whatshername wasn't perhaps quite so bad after all, behind that rather tiresome manner; appearances, inevitably, deceive. One got the impression, too, of someone who'd maybe had a bit of a rough time. "Well, it's a world that includes all sorts, like most. And it brings you up against life, I suppose, with all that that implies."

The respect with which these banalities were received made him feel a little cheap. In compensation, he told her an anecdote about a case in which he had once been involved; a *crime passionel* involving an apparently wronged husband who had turned out in fact to be the villain of the piece. "A mealy-mouthed fellow, and as plausible as you like, but apparently he'd been systematically persecuting her for years." Moira Lukes nodded sagely. "People absolutely are not what they seem to be."

"Well," said the judge. "Yes and no. On the other hand, plenty of people give themselves away as soon as they open their mouths."

"Oh, goodness," said Moira Lukes. "Now I'll feel I daren't utter a word ever again."

"I had in mind those I come across professionally rather than in private life."

"Ah, then you think I'm safe?"

"Now, whatever could you have to conceal?" said the judge amiably. A bell went. "I wonder where Marjorie's got to. I suppose we'd better start going back in."

Moira Lukes sighed. She turned those large eyes upon him and creased them once again at the corners. "Well, this has been so nice. I'm sure we'll run into each other again over the weekend. But do bear in mind that I'm in the East Sussex phone book. I remember that case I read about was in Brighton – if you're ever judging there again and want a few hours' retreat on your own, do pop over and have a drink." She smiled once more, and walked quickly away into the crowd.

The judge stood for a moment, looking after her. He realised with surprise that he had been on the receiving end of what is generally known as a pass. He realised also that he was finding it difficult to sort out exactly what he felt about this; a rational response and his natural judgement of people (he didn't in fact all that much care for the woman) fought with more reprehensible feelings and a certain complacency (so one wasn't a total old buffer just yet). In this state of internal conflict he made his way back into the concert hall, where he found Marjorie already in her seat.

"What on earth happened to you?"

"Sorry," she said cheerfully. "There was an awful queue in the Ladies and by the time I got out it wasn't worth coming to find you. How did you make out with our friend?"

The judge grunted, and applied himself to the programme. The lights went down, the conductor reappeared, the audience sank into silence . . . But the music, somehow, had lost its compulsion; he was aware now of too much that was external – that he could achieve no satisfactory position for his legs, that he had slight indigestion, that the chap in front of him kept moving his head. Beside him, he could see Marjorie's face, rapt. The evening, somehow, had been corrupted.

The next morning was even more seraphic than the one before. "Today," said Marjorie, "we are going to sit on the beach and bask. We may even venture into the sea."

"That sounds a nice idea." The judge had thought during the night of the little episode with that woman and, in the process, a normal balance of mind had returned; he felt irritated – though more with himself than with her – that it had interfered with his enjoyment of the concert. It was with some annoyance, therefore, that he spotted her now across the hotel dining-room, with the sister, lifting her hand in a little finger-waggling wave of greeting.

"What's the matter?" said Marjorie, with marital insight. "Oh . . . Her. Well, I'll leave you to hide behind the paper. I'm going upstairs to get sorted out for the beach."

He was half-way through the Home News page when he felt her standing over him. Alone. The sister, evidently, had been disposed of.

"Another heavenly day. Aren't we lucky! All on your own? I saw your wife bustling off . . ." She continued to stand, her glance drifting now towards the coffee pot at the judge's elbow.

11

I am supposed, he thought, to say sit down and join me – have a cup of coffee. And he felt again that quiver of the antennae and knew now the reason. Marjorie does indeed bustle, her walk is rather inelegant, but it is not for you to say so, or to subtly denigrate a person I happen to love. He rattled, slightly, his newspaper. "We're off to the beach shortly."

"Oh, lovely. I daresay we'll go down there later. I wonder . . . Goodness, I don't know if I ought to ask you this or not . . ." She hesitated, prettily, seized, it seemed with sudden diffidence. "Oh, I'll be brave. The thing is, I have this tiresome problem about a flat in London I'm buying, something to do with the leasehold that I simply do not follow, and I just do not have absolute faith in the man who's dealing with it for me – the solicitor, you know – *could* I pick your brains about it at some point?"

The judge, impassive, gazed up at her.

"I don't mean *now* – not in the middle of your holiday weekend. My sister was noticing your address in the hotel register and believe it or not my present flat is only a few minutes away. What would be lovely would be if you could spare an hour or so to look in for a drink on your way home one evening – and your wife too of course only it might be awfully boring for her if you're going to brief me. Is that the right word? Would it be an imposition? When you're on your own like I am you are so very much at the mercy of . . ." – she sighed – "people, the system, I don't know what . . . Sometimes I get quite panic-stricken."

I doubt that, thought the judge. He put the newspaper down. "Mrs Lukes . . ."

"Oh, Moira . . . please."

He cleared his throat. "Conveyancing, as it happens, is not my field. Anything I said might quite possibly be misleading. The only sensible advice I can give is to change your solicitor if you feel lack of confidence in him."

Her eyes flickered; that look of honest appeal dimmed, suddenly. "Oh . . . I see. Well, I daresay you're right. I must do that, then. I shouldn't have asked. But of course the invitation stands, whenever you're free."

"How kind," said the judge coolly. He picked up his paper again and looked at her over the top of it; their eyes met in understanding. And he flinched a little at her expression; it was the look of hatred he had seen from time to time, over the years, across a courtroom, on the face in the dock.

"Have a *lovely* day," said Moira Lukes. Composure had returned; she gleamed, and wrinkled her eyes, and was gone. Well, thought the judge, there's no love lost there, now. But it had to be done, once and for all. He folded the paper and went in search of Marjorie.

She was packing a beach-bag with costumes and towels. The judge, unlocking the suitcase, took out a stack of the pornographic magazines and pushed them into the bottom of the bag. "Oh, lor," said Marjorie, "I'd forgotten about them. Must you?"

" 'Fraid so. The case resumes tomorrow. It's the usual business of going through them for degrees of obscenity. There are some books too."

"I'll help you," said Marjorie. "There – greater love hath no woman . . ."

The beach was agreeably uncrowded. Family parties were dotted in clumps about the sand; children and dogs skittered in and out of the surf; gulls floated above the water and a party of small wading birds scurried back and forth before the advancing waves like blown leaves. The judge, who enjoyed a bit of unstrenuous bird-watching, sat observing them with affection. The weather, this particularly delectable manifestation of the physical world and the uncomplicated relish of the people and animals around him had induced a state of general benignity. Marjorie, organising the rug and wind-screen, said, "All right?" "All right?" he replied. They smiled at each other, appreciating the understatement.

Marjorie, after a while, resolutely swam. The judge, more craven, followed her to the water's edge and observed. As they walked back up the beach together he saw suddenly that Moira Lukes and her sister were encamped not far off. She glanced at him and then immediately away. Now, at midday, the beach was becoming more occupied, though not disturbingly so. A family had established itself close to the Braines' pitch: young parents with a baby in a pram and a couple of older children now deeply engaged in the initial stages of sandcastle construction. The judge, who had also made a sandcastle or two in his time, felt an absurd urge to lend a hand; the basic design, he could see, was awry and would give trouble before long. The mother, a fresh-faced young woman, came padding across the sand to ask Marjorie for the loan of a tin-opener. They chatted for a moment; the young woman carried the baby on her hip. "That sort of thing," said Marjorie, sitting down again, "can still make me broody, even at my time of life." She too watched the sandcastle-building; presently she rummaged in the picnic basket and withdrew a plastic beaker. "Turrets," she explained to the judge, a little guiltily. "You can never do a good job with a bucket . . ." The children received her offering with rewarding glee; the parents gratefully smiled; the sandcastle rose, more stylish.

The judge sighed, and delved in the beach bag. "To work, I suppose," he said. Around them, the life of the beach had settled into a frieze, as though the day were eternal: little sprawled groups of people, the great arc of

the horizon against which stood the grey shapes of two
far-away ships, like cut-outs, the surface animation of running dogs and children and someone's straw hat, tossed
hither and thither by the breeze that had sprung up.

The judge and his wife sat with a pile of magazines each.
Marjorie said, "This is a pretty gruesome collection. Can I
borrow your hankie, my glasses keep getting salted over."

The judge turned over pages, and occasionally made
some notes. Nothing he saw surprised him; from time to
time he found himself examining the faces that belonged to
the bodies displayed, as though in search of explanations.
But they seemed much like any other faces; so presumably
were the bodies.

Marjorie said, "Cup of tea? Tell me, why are words
capable of so much greater obscenity than pictures?" She
was glancing through a book, or something that passed as
such.

"That, I imagine, is why people have always gone in for
burning them, though usually for quite other reasons."

It was as the judge was reaching out to take the mug of tea
from her that the wind came. It came in a great wholesome
gust, flinging itself along the beach with a cloud of blown
sand and flying plastic bags. It sent newspapers into the air
like great flapping birds and spun a spotted football along
the water's edge as though it were a top. It lifted rugs and
pushed over deckchairs. It snatched the magazines from the
judge's lap and from Marjorie's and bore them away across
the sand in a helter-skelter whirl of colourful pages, dropping
them down only to grab them again and fling them here and
there: at the feet of a stout lady snoozing in a deckchair, into
the pram of the neighbouring family's baby, onto people's
towels and Sunday newspapers.

Marjorie said "Oh, *lor* . . ."

They got up. They began, separately, to tour the beach in

pursuit of what the wind had taken. The judge found himself, absurdly, feeling foolish because he had left his jacket on his chair and was plodding along the sand in shirt-sleeves (no tie, either) and tweed trousers. The lady in the deckchair woke and put out a hand to quell the magazine that was wrapping itself around her leg. "Yours?" she said amiably, looking up at the judge, and as she handed him the thing it fell open and for a moment her eyes rested on the central spread, the *pièce de resistance*; her expression changed, rubbed out as it were by amazement, and she looked again at the judge for an instant, and became busy with the knitting on her lap.

Marjorie, stumping methodically along, picked up one magazine and then another, tucking them under her arm. She turned and saw that the children had observed the crisis, abandoned their sandcastle and were scurrying here and there, collecting as though involved in a treasure hunt. The mother, too, had risen and was shaking the sand from a magazine that had come to rest against the wheels of the pram. As Marjorie reached her the little girl ran up with an armful. "Good girl, Sharon," said the mother, and the child – six, perhaps, or seven – virtuously beamed and held out to Marjorie the opened pages of the magazine she held. She looked at it and the mother looked at it and Marjorie looked and the child said, "Are those flowers?". "No, my dear," said Marjorie sadly. "They aren't flowers", and she turned away before she could meet the eyes of the young mother.

The judge collected a couple from a man who handed them over with a wink, and another from a boy who stared at him expressionless, and then he could not find any more. He walked back to their pitch. Marjorie was shoving things into the beach bag. "Shall we go?" she said, and the judge nodded.

It was as they were folding the rug that Moira Lukes came up. She wore neatly creased cotton trousers and walked with a spring. "Yours, apparently," she said; she held the magazine out between a finger and thumb, as though with tongs, and dropped it onto the sand. She looked straight at the judge. "How awfully true," she said, "that people are not what they seem to be." Satisfaction flowed from her; she glanced for an instant, at Marjorie, as though checking that she had heard, and walked away.

The Braines, in silence, completed the assembly of their possessions. Marjorie carried the rug and the picnic basket and the judge bore the beach bag and the wind-screen. They trudged the long expanse of the beach, watched, now, with furtive interest by various eyes.

Venice, now and then

"VENICE!" SHE SAID, getting up, crossing the room. "Of course! The Doge's Palace and the Campanile. It's nice. Where did you get it?"

"I saw it in a junk shop."

London traffic rumbled beyond the window. "Yes," she went on. "Doesn't it take you back! We went over to that church once, the picture must have been done from that side. San – San . . ."

"Santa Maria della Salute."

"That's it." She stabbed a finger on the glass. "That's where I bought the fluorescent necklace. There – under that arch."

He peered, as though the past should be made manifest. "Really? I thought it was in the square. How things get distorted. What I remember is the heat at night. Like being in warm soup."

There are long quivering ribbons of light on the water. A tanker passes, huge black bulk eclipsing churches and palaces, bigger than any of this, sending ridge after ridge of waves to slosh against the quay, against the tethered boats. To and fro the people go, hundreds of them, to and fro, walking and talking, us with them: Liz and I and Belinda and Alan. Here today, gone tomorrow – well, next

19

week. Has everyone in the world passed this way, at some time or another? A place is a receptacle; perhaps only places exist, not people.

I should like to eat. I catch the others up. Liz is buying something from a man with a tray of postcards, scarves, ties. Alan holds Belinda's hand. Liz says, "Look, I couldn't resist it! Fix it for me, James."

They curl round people's necks like glow-worms. I say, "I must have one!" Alan and Belinda watch, smiling; Alan wears a blue shirt, his hair is crimped by sea and salt. James fastens the necklace, he fastens it to the hairs at the back of my neck and I complain. "Il faut souffrir," says Alan, "pour etre belle." We sit down at a pavement restaurant, laughing. There are live fish in a tank, and shafts of light furry with insects.

"How much?" she said. "Twenty-five – that's not bad, I suppose, for nowadays. Actually I'd have hung it over the desk. If I was consulted. By the way you haven't said what you think of the new hair-do." She turned her head from side to side, displaying.

"There's less of it," he observed at last, cautiously.

"Of course there's less of it, you nit, that's the idea."

"Where was it," he said, "that those Carpaccios were?"

"O Carpaccios, where art thou?" sings Belinda. "Wherever art thee – thou – they?" She leans over a parapet. "Two plastic bottles, seventeen lettuce leaves, something horrible I don't want to know about, someone's T-shirt, yesterday's paper . . ."

James stands with the map in his hand, scowling. He turns the map this way and that; he aligns map and street; he squints to right and left; he tries to marry print and the real world. We hang about.

20

"Perhaps," suggests Alan, "we should give them a miss. We're back where we were ten minutes ago, I rather think, James."

And James fusses that no, no, we can't possibly miss them, they are one of the things, the book says, and just a sec he's got it now, if we go up there and then right . . .

We follow him. "Carpaccio, Carpaccio," sings Belinda. "Wherefore art thou, Carpaccio?"

We wander through a trompe l'oeil landscape in which streets run slap into buildings and canals, in which people vanish into walls, in which a square has no visible exit. We pick our way from here to there, from there to here. I shunt my dark glasses off and on, on and off; we plunge from heat to cool murky interiors. We stand in attentive observation; we switchback over bridges. I shell out money into the hands of a grumpy custodian; we file into the hot dim room. Outside, men are drilling the street. The man closes the door and the noise is quenched. "Aren't they small?" says Liz. "I imagined enormous, somehow."

"Oh, goodness," she said. "San something or other. Do I get a drink, James dear, I'm whacked."

He stood beside her, fiddling with bottles. "Do you ever, in fact, see anything of Alan?"

"I work in the same organization as Alan. Now, as then. Of course I see Alan. From time to time. Alan has got a bit stout. Alan has moved to Fulham."

"I just wondered."

"Actually," she said, "I like Alan, still. Ah well."

Alan, who has nice manners, hands me into the boat. He holds my elbow, steadying. He says, "Here, give me the bag. O.K.?" We have been dropped out of the sky into an apricot evening. The sky is apricot and the amazing horizon and the quivering molten air. Belinda says, "Oh dear, I should have been to the ladies at the

21

airport, I wonder how long it takes?" Alan sits beside her. "Control yourself, my girl," he says, and he smiles across at me. "Well, far cry from Whitehall now, eh?" I look round for James, but James has gone to sit at the end, the prow, the whatever it is. He stares all round; he is trying to get his bearings; James likes to know where he is, always.

We dash through a world that is manifestly circular, leaving a carven white wake; we fly across this disc of water rimmed with land, an indeterminate ring of substance that resolves itself here and there into a scribble of cranes and chimneys, a sequence of domes and towers. Pewter clouds lie all around the horizon, with bellies of lemon and gold and silver. Liz shouts into the throbbing air; I cannot hear a word. I lean forward. She bawls, "Isn't it fun! I'm so glad we didn't take the bus." I nod.

"Hmn . . ." he said. "I don't know about time clarifying things. What it does do is add something."

"Years?" she suggested. "Grey hairs?"

"I can't see any. Or did they cut them all off?"

"Beast. Belinda, now, is just the same."

"I can't," he said, "remember Belinda any more. Belinda then. Odd, that."

"Oh, I can. That bag she was always leaving behind in cafés. Some special sunburn stuff. Graham Greene."

Belinda is reading Brighton Rock. *"It's ages since I read that," I say. "He dies in the end, doesn't he? The boy. Pinky. He has this bottle of acid and . . ."*

"You wretch!" cries Belinda. "Now you've told me what happens. Now you've spoilt it." "Not spoilt it," corrects Alan. "You can still enjoy it, it's the same book." "No it isn't," says Belinda. "I know how it ends now. Everything is changed when you know what's coming." "Sorry," I say.

22

"Tiresome girl," complains Belinda. She puts her glasses back on; she reads.

I pick my way past tables to where Belinda sits, reading. She looks up. "Oh," she says. "James. Alan's just checking on those ferry times. Wretched Liz has told me how my book ends so she's gone to buy the Sunday papers, as a penance. Tea or coffee?" And she gazes at me, eyes screwed up against the brightness in a face I can no longer see, because it no longer exists, the face of Belinda then, the face of Alan's wife Belinda. I sit opposite her on an uncomfortable metal chair with patterned seat; I can feel metal and absence of metal through the cotton of my trousers; I sit there wondering how it is possible to feel a pattern. Belinda talks about a film at the Notting Hill Classic.

"It could do," she said, "with a nicer frame."

"Ah. Possibly."

"And a bit of a clean-up. Shall I do the glass? Or would that be considered forward?"

He reflected. "I should wait, maybe."

"Scuola di something. Where the Carpaccios were. Scuola di . . . di . . ."

The ceiling is all red and gold. My sandal hurts where the strap has rubbed. There is this fearful drilling noise and then snap! it is cut off, turned down to a mumble, and instead there is a voice in German, level, instructive, impassive. We move, James and Belinda and Alan and I, around the room keeping as far as we can from the guided German party, superior in our unconducted independence. We are absorbed; we forget, perhaps, about each other.

I look up and I see James stand beside Belinda. I can see them still: my tall stooping brother James and Belinda in a flowered

23

*cotton skirt and a pink top, people who do not know each other very
well, staring at a painting.*

*I stand beside Belinda, who is the friend of my sister, whose
husband Alan is also the friend of my sister, and I look at the
picture. I can see it now; the man's face turned to the light, the little
white dog, the book fallen to the floor. Belinda says, "St. Augustine
in his study." And then, "The dog is just like our neighbour's dog."
I smile politely at Belinda; I look down at her: I see a pleasant
woman, plumpish. As though through a glass, darkly.*

"I can't stay long, but I'll have a top up if you're pressing
me. Is it for something special – the picture?"
    "Something special?"
    "Birthday?"
    "Oh no." He looked again at it, in surprise, as though it
were unexpectedly there. "Nothing special, no. Just that it
caught my eye. You know . . . Struck one as pleasant.
Familiar. Did I pay too much?"
    "Familiar? Well, yes, I suppose. Familiar, I mean – not
paying too much. And yet you know I could have sworn
that was *there.*" She tapped, again, the glass. "Remember
the thunderstorm?"

*Lightning flares. Wild, operatic lightning. The buildings are pro-
jected against sculptural cloudshapes from which surely must ride
forth Valkyrie or seraphim or a trio singing Mozart. It is quite
unreal, as unreal as the cathedral, the palace, the campanile, all of
which must have been erected yesterday in mockery of what is
claimed. All is a stage-set, as are the people extras, a great
Hollywood army of extras that ebbs and flows around the square,
up and down, to and fro, this way and that. Should one applaud?
Or is the climax yet to come?*

James suddenly claps his hands. He stands there in shirt-sleeves clapping his hands. "Your brother," says Alan, "is determined to be the original eccentric Englishman." He smiles, benignly; he is older than we are, sometimes there creeps in a licensed avuncular note. And now there is fork lightning against sheet lightning, a stunning effect, a metallic sizzle against the great white flare, and far away the landscape growls, off-stage. "It isn't," says Alan, "happening here at all. Over the Dolomites, I reckon. Miles away." And Belinda is uneasy; it's going to pour, she claims, any minute now, it's going to come chucking down and anyway lightning always makes me queasy, suppose it hit one of those pinnacles, we'd all be . . . She scuttles round us, like a sheepdog, chivvying. She chivvies James, who stands now with arms folded, intently appreciative, and James gives one last clap or two and smiles, amiable, detached, and we all move away, back to the hotel.

"Things," he said, "are so inconstant. That's the trouble."

"Buildings don't move. If it isn't where I think it was then it isn't. Places stay the same."

"True," he agreed. "It's nice there's something to rely on."

"Where are the children? There's the most unearthly hush."

He stared at her over the rim of the glass. "Let me see now . . . I was told. Out. Out at . . . a music lesson?"

"I do envy you," she said, "that capacity for insulation."

"It's been put to the test these last few years, I must admit."

"They are perfectly delightful, as children go."

"So I'm told."

"How odd it is," she said, "to think that then, in Venice, they simply didn't exist."

"Inconceivable," he said, "or unconceived?"

"Both. If anyone had suggested then . . ."

25

"Oh, quite. Astonishment would have laid us flat. It would have spoiled," he went on, "a rather nice little holiday."

Beneath the gleaming ceilings shuffles the crowd, necks askance, speaking with tongues. A river of people, self-perpetuating, surely, there cannot be so many different *people passing this way. In at one end, out at the other, drifting through. I find a point where I can sit before a tumultuous canvas; the painted people too are legion, saints and Christs and Marys and those who weep and those who watch. I consult the book. I look up again and Liz is there, plumping herself down beside me. "Do you like them?" she says, and I consider the great spread before me, the great complex glittering spread. "Not that, silly," she says. "Them. Alan and Belinda." I reply that it is too hot for judgements and in any case I am hungry.*

"Your brother," says Belinda, "is terribly earnest about looking at things. Not," she adds hastily, "that he isn't sweet. He puts us all to shame. Dare we, do you think, move him on?" And we look across the room at James, screened from us by people, an ebb and flow of bodies through which we glimpse James sitting with his book, his now battered book, relating this to that and that to this. I go and sit by James and James tells me about annunciations and crucifixions and resurrections.

"Spoiled? It might have made it more interesting. It would have added a certain something, you must admit."

"Spoiled," he said firmly.

"There's the front door."

He took a third glass. "Let's hope I shan't be thought to have been extravagant."

"Oh – the picture. Of course not. She'll love it, I should think. Scuola di San Giorgio – there, I've got it! Now I'm

26

happy. It's maddening when you can't remember something right."

"Was it?" he said. "I daresay. I'm never good on names. There was a dragon, wasn't there, and St. Jerome with his lion."

A most humane lion. And fleeing affronted figures and greens and reds overlaid with a hazy gold, the sunshine of another century, it seems to be. I stand in a pleasant trance of observation, thinking of nothing, a pair of eyes, no more. I feel space occupied beside me; I glance; Belinda is sharing St. Augustine – his window, his dog, his fallen book.

We are linked by the permanence of the painting, standing forever in a hot dim room; the painting is still there, in the mind's eye, but Belinda has gone, Belinda then, rubbed out by what has come since, Belinda cannot be retrieved.

Well, I think, it's as well we did find it, James was right, or James's blessed book, they aren't to be missed. And I wander round the room, homing on this one and then that. I sit down on a bench and try to do something about my sandal strap, about my foot with its red itching groove. I stuff a tissue in and go back to the dragon painting. I look round for the others and see Alan buying postcards, waiting patiently in a cluster of people, his hands in his pockets.

Belinda is standing beside James at the other side of the room. James stoops a little to hear what she says; she tilts her head up at him. I can see them still, but they are overlaid with the wisdoms of now; James looks down at Belinda, he smiles, he smiles at his wife.

27

Grow old along with me,
the best is yet to be

"Oh, I don't know . . ." said Sarah. "Decisions, decisions. I hate them. I mean, one of the things that bothers me is – would I stop being *me*? Would I change. If we did."

She wore dungarees in pale turquoise, and a white T-shirt. She drove the Fiat hunched forward over the steering-wheel. Her face was engulfed by large reflecting sun-glasses across which flew hedges, trees, a passing car. "It's rather gorgeous round here, isn't it? Half-asleep, as though nothing happens in a hundred years."

Tony said, "We both might. It's a significant step in a relationship – that's the point of it, I suppose."

"And the point of waiting. Thinking about it. Not rushing."

"Not that we have."

"Quite. Shall we stop and eat soon?"

"Yes – when there's a reasonable pub."

Gloucestershire unreeled at either side: dark green, straw-coloured, unpopulated. Trees drooped in the fields; a village was still and silent except for a lorry throbbing outside a shop. High summer gripped the landscape; birds twitched from hedge to hedge.

"Half the time," said Sarah, "it doesn't crop up. One sort

CORRUPTION

of puts it out of one's mind – there are too many other things
to think of. And then it begins to nag. We've got to either do
it or not do it."

"We've been not doing it for three years, darling."

"I know, I know. But all the same, it looms."

"We are actually," he said, "better off, from a tax point of
view, unmarried. Since your rise. We went into that in the
winter – remember?"

"What about this – Free House, Bar Snacks. How much
better off, exactly?"

"Oh, lord, I don't know. Hundreds, anyway."

She turned the car into the pub yard. "It's a point, then.
Ma keeps saying, what happens if there's a baby? And I say
well that would of course put a different complexion on
things but *until* we are absolutely free to choose. The trouble
is that dear ma thinks I'm on the shelf at twenty-six. I keep
saying, there aren't shelves now."

The woman behind the bar watched them come in, a
good-looking young couple, in the pink of health, not short
of money, the kind of people who know their way around.
She served them lagers and chicken salad, and noted Sarah's
neat figure, not an ounce in the wrong place, which induced
vague discontent. I'm dieting, she thought, as from Monday
I am, I swear to God. She observed also Tony's tanned
forearms, below the rolled sleeves of an indefinably modish
shirt, like blokes in colour supp. ads. Thirtyish, nice voice.
He didn't look at her, pocketing the change, turning away
with the plates. She watched them settle in the corner by the
window, sitting close, talking. In love, presumably, lucky
so-and-so's.

"Tax is certainly a point," said Sarah. "Getting dependent
on each other is another. Look at Tom and Alison. But one
still feels that eventually we're going to have to make some
kind of decision. You can have my pickled onion."

"Lots of people don't. Decide, I mean. Look at Blake and Susan."

"I don't want to look at Blake and Susan. Blake's forty-two, did you know that? And anyway he's *been* married. Oh, isn't it all difficult? We decided no baby, barring accidents, at least not yet, and that was one decision. Thank God for the pill, I suppose. I mean, imagine when they just *happened*."

"They still do sometimes. Look at Maggie."

"Oh, Maggie meant to, for goodness sake. That baby was no accident. It was psychological."

They ate, for a while, in silence. At the bar middle-aged men, locals, sporadically conversed, out of kilter like clocks ticking at different speeds. The woman wiped glasses. A commercial traveller came in and ordered a steak and kidney with chips. On the wall, hand-written posters advertised a Bring and Buy, a Darby and Joan Outing. Tony stacked their empty plates. "Not exactly the hub of the universe, this."

"It's rather sweet. Laurie Lee country. I used to adore that book – what's-it-called? – we did it for O-levels. Sex in the hedges and all that. O.K. – I'll find the loo and we'll get moving. Where are we, by the way, I've lost track?"

When she came back he had the map book open on his knee. "Let's have a look, there might be something to go and see. Oh, goodness, there is – we're not far from Deerhurst. Oh, we must see Deerhurst. You know – Saxon church, very special."

"Right you are. Do we have Pevsner?"

"On the back shelf of the car. What luck – I never realised Deerhurst was hereabouts."

"Aren't you a clever girl?" he said, patting her knee. "Knowing about Saxon churches."

The woman behind the bar, watching them, thought,

31

yes, that's how it is when you're like that. Can't keep your hands off each other. Ah well. "How's the back, John?" she said. "That stuff I told you about do any good?" The young couple were getting up now, slinging sweaters about their shoulders, leaving without a backwards glance. People passing through, going off into other lives. Young intense lives. "What? Oh, thanks very much – I'll have a lager and lime. Cheers, John."

"Drive or navigate?" said Sarah, in the car park. "You're better with the map than I am, and it's all side roads to this church. I'll tell you one thing – if we do get married it's not going to be any flipping church business. That's what ma's got her eye on, you realise."

"There'd have to be some sort of do."

"We could have it at the flat. Cheaper. The do, I mean. And registry office. But it's all a bit academic, until we actually decide something. Do I go left or right?"

Signposts fingered towards slothful hinterlands. Cars glittered between the hedges, sparks of colour in a world of green and fawn. On the edge of a village, washing-lines held up stiff shapes of clothes, slumping pink and yellow sheets, a rank of nappies. A man scraped around young cabbages with a hoe.

"Corfu," said Tony, "was livelier."

"I thought we agreed never again a package holiday. Anyway, it's the new car this year instead."

"This is our fourth holiday together, Sarah."

"Cor . . . Hey – you're not directing me. That sign said Deerhurst."

"Sorry. My mind was on other things. Incidentally, what started us off on this marriage discussion? Today, I mean."

"I can't remember. Oh yes I can – it was you talking about this aunt of yours. Will you have to go to the wedding, by the way?"

"I hope not. I'd be the only person there under fifty, I should imagine. No – hearty good wishes over the phone and that kind of thing."

"It's nice for her," said Sarah charitably. "At that age. If a bit kind of fake, if you see what I mean."

"Yes. But for that generation there wouldn't be any alternative."

They nodded, sombrely.

"Here we are," said Sarah. "And this must be where you leave cars. Good – there's no one else there. I hate looking at churches when there's anyone else. Where's Pevsner? We're going to do this place properly – it's supposed to be important."

They advanced into the churchyard. The church, squatting amid yews, seemed almost derisive in its antiquity, tethered to something dark and incomprehensible, uncaring, too far away to be understood. Its stone was blurred, its shapes strange and unlovely. Gravestones drowned in grass. An aeroplane, unseen, rumbled across the milky sky.

"'. . . tall narrow nave of the C8'," Tony read. "Seven hundred and something. Jesus! That makes you think, doesn't it?"

"There's this famous sculpture thing over the door. An animal head. That's it, I suppose. Goodness, isn't it all sinister?"

They stood in silence. "Things that are so incredibly old," Sarah went on, "just leave you feeling respectful. I mean, that they're there at all."

They went into the church. Tony took a few steps down the nave. "Yes. I know what you mean. Even more so inside. All this stone standing for so long" – he gestured at piers, crossing arch, narrow uncompromising windows. "Read Pevsner," instructed Sarah. "I like to understand what I'm looking at." They toured the building, side by side, heads cocked from book to architectural feature, understanding.

The church door, which they had closed behind them, burst open. The sound made them both jump. Turning, they saw a man who stood framed in the gush of light from without: a tall man in tweed jacket and baggy-kneed trousers, an odd prophetic-looking figure with a mane of white hair, like a more robust version of the aged Bertrand Russell. A memorable person, who stood for a moment staring wildly round the church, at Sarah and Tony for one dismissive instant, and who then strode down the aisle searching, apparently, the pillars, and then back to the entrance and out, slamming the door.

"The vicar?" said Tony, after a moment.

"No. Frankly. That was no vicar. Funny to storm out like that, though. This place *vaut le detour*, as *Michelin* says."

"P'raps he's seen it already."

"Presumably." Sarah turned back to Pevsner. "Apparently there's this other carving outside, round at the back, we'd better go and find it. We've done the rest, I think."

She led the way out of the church and round the side, through the long grass and the leaning grave-stones. And came, thus, upon them first.

In the angle of a buttress, up against the wall of the church. The man, the white-haired tall man, his back now turned. Turned because he was locked in an embrace, a succulent sexual embrace (the sound, just, of mouths – the impression of loins pushed together) with a woman little of whom could be seen as, eyes averted, Sarah scurried past, followed a few paces behind by Tony. Both of them at once seeing, and quickly looking away. Seeing of the man his tweed back and his mane of yellow-white hair and of the woman – well, little except an impression of blue denim skirt and plimsolls. And more white hair: crisp curly grey-white hair.

They achieved the back of the church and stood peering up at the wall.

"I can't see this sculpture," said Sarah (voice firm, ordinary, not lowered, rather loud indeed). "It's supposed to be a Virgin – ah, that must be it. Right up just under the window there."

When they came back past the buttress the couple were gone. The churchyard was quite empty. The whole place, which had briefly rocked, had sunk back into its lethargy. That crackling startling charge of passion had dissipated into the stagnant air of the summer afternoon. It was three o'clock, and felt as if it forever would be. Somewhere beyond the hedge a tractor ground across a field.

"Let's go," said Sarah brightly. "I think I've had Deerhurst."

The car was no longer alone. Two others, now, were parked alongside. Sarah whipped the key into the lock and opened the door. She plumped down into the driving-seat. "You know what? That was an assignation we stumbled into."

"So it would seem."

"Where are they now, do you imagine?"

Tony shrugged.

Sarah started the engine. She said with sudden violence, "You know, it was a bit revolting. They were seventy if they were a day."

Tony nodded. Embarrassment filled the car.

The darkness out there

SHE WALKED THROUGH flowers, the girl, oxeye daisies and vetch and cow parsley, keeping to the track at the edge of the field. She could see the cottage in the distance, shrugged down into the dip beyond the next hedge. Mrs Rutter, Pat had said, Mrs Rutter at Nether Cottage, you don't know her, Sandra? She's a dear old thing, all on her own, of course, we try to keep an eye. A wonky leg after her op and the home help's off with a bad back this week. So could you make that your Saturday afternoon session, dear? Lovely. There'll be one of the others, I'm not sure who.

Pat had a funny eye, a squint, so that her glance swerved away from you as she talked. And a big chest jutting under washed-out jerseys. Are people who help other people always not very nice-looking? Very busy being busy; always in a rush. You didn't get people like Mrs Carpenter at the King's Arms running the Good Neighbours Club. People with platinum highlights and spike heel suede boots.

She looked down at her own legs, the girl, bare brown legs brushing through the grass, polleny summer grass that glinted in the sun.

She hoped it would be Susie, the other person. Or Liz. They could have a good giggle, doing the floors and that. Doing her washing, this old Mrs Rutter.

They were all in the Good Neighbours Club, her set at school. Quite a few of the boys, too. It had become a sort of craze, the thing to do. They were really nice, some of the old people. The old folks, Pat called them. Pat had done the notice in the Library: *Come and have fun giving a helping hand to the old folks. Adopt a granny.* And the joky cartoon drawing of a dear old bod with specs on the end of her nose and a shawl. One or two of the old people had been a bit sharp about that.

The track followed the hedge round the field to the gate and the plank bridge over the stream. The dark reach of the spinney came right to the gate there so that she would have to walk by the edge of it with the light suddenly shutting off, the bare wide sky of the field. Packer's End.

You didn't go by yourself through Packer's End if you could help it, not after tea-time, anyway. A German plane came down in the war and the aircrew were killed and there were people who'd heard them talking still, chattering in German on their radios, voices coming out of the trees, nasty, creepy. People said.

She kept to the track, walking in the flowers with corn running in the wind between her and the spinney. She thought suddenly of blank-eyed helmeted heads, looking at you from among branches. She wouldn't go in there for a thousand pounds, not even in bright day like now, with nothing coming out of the dark slab of trees but birdsong – blackbirds and thrushes and robins and that. It was a rank place, all whippy saplings and brambles and a gully with a dumped mattress and bedstead and an old fridge. And, somewhere, presumably, the crumbling rusty scraps of metal and cloth and . . . Bones?

It was all right out here in the sunshine. Fine. She stopped to pick grass stems out of her sandal; she saw the neat print of the strap-marks against her sunburn, pink-white on

38

brown. Somebody had said she had pretty feet, once; she looked at them, clean and plump and neat on the grass. A ladybird crawled across a toe.

When they were small, six and seven and eight, they'd been scared stiff of Packer's End. Then, they hadn't known about the German plane. It was different things then; witches and wolves and tigers. Sometimes they'd go there for a dare, several of them, skittering over the field and into the edge of the trees, giggling and shrieking, not too far in, just far enough for it to be scary, for the branch shapes to look like faces and clawed hands, for the wolves to rustle and creep in the greyness you couldn't quite see into, the clotted shifting depths of the place.

But after, lying on your stomach at home on the hearthrug watching telly with the curtains drawn and the dark shut out it was cosy to think of Packer's End, where you weren't.

After they were twelve or so the witches and wolves went away. Then it was the German plane. And other things too. You didn't know who there might be around, in woods and places. Like stories in the papers. Girl attacked on lonely road. Police hunt rapist. There was this girl, people at school said, this girl sometime back who'd been biking along the field path and these two blokes had come out of Packer's End. They'd had a knife, they'd threatened to carve her up, there wasn't anything she could do, she was at their mercy. People couldn't remember what her name was, exactly, she didn't live round here any more. Two enormous blokes, sort of gyspy types.

She put her sandal back on. She walked through the thicker grass by the hedge and felt it drag at her legs and thought of swimming in warm seas. She put her hand on the top of her head and her hair was hot from the sun, a dry burning cap. One day, this year, next year sometime, she

39

would go to places like on travel brochures and run into a blue sea. She would fall in love and she would get a good job and she would have one of those new Singers that do zig-zag stitch and make an embroidered silk coat.

One day.

Now, she would go to this old Mrs Rutter's and have a bit of a giggle with Susie and come home for tea and wash her hair. She would walk like this through the silken grass with the wind seething the corn and the secret invisible life of birds beside her in the hedge. She would pick a blue flower and examine its complexity of pattern and petal and wonder what it was called and drop it. She would plunge her face into the powdery plate of an elderflower and smell cat, tom-cat, and sneeze and scrub her nose with the back of her hand. She would hurry through the gate and over the stream because that was a bit too close to Packer's End for comfort and she would . . .

He rose from the plough beyond the hedge.

She screamed.

"Christ!" she said. "Kerry Stevens you stupid so-and-so, what d'you want to go and do that for you give me the fright of my life."

He grinned. "I seen you coming. Thought I might as well wait."

Not Susie. Not Liz either. Kerry Stevens from Richmond Way. Kerry Stevens that none of her lot reckoned much on, with his black licked-down hair and slitty eyes. Some people you only have to look at to know they're not up to much.

"Didn't know you were in the Good Neighbours."

He shrugged. They walked in silence. He took out an aero bar, broke off a bit, offered it. She said oh, thanks. They went chewing towards the cottage, the cottage where old Mrs Rutter with her wonky leg would be ever so pleased to see them because they were really sweet, lots of the old people. Ever so grateful the old poppets, was what Pat said, not that you'd put it quite like that yourself.

"Just give it a push, the door. It sticks, see. That's it."

She seemed composed of circles, a cottage-loaf of a woman, with a face below which chins collapsed one into another, a creamy smiling pool of a face in which her eyes snapped and darted.

"Tea, my duck?" she said. "Tea for the both of you? I'll put us a kettle on."

The room was stuffy. It had a gaudy lino floor with the pattern rubbed away in front of the sink and round the table; the walls were cluttered with old calendars and pictures torn from magazines; there was a smell of cabbage. The alcove by the fireplace was filled with china ornaments: big-eyed flop-eared rabbits and beribboned kittens and flowery milkmaids and a pair of naked chubby children wearing daisy chains.

The woman hauled herself from a sagging armchair. She glittered at them from the stove, manoeuvring cups, propping herself against the draining-board. "What's your names, then? Sandra and Kerry. Well, you're a pretty girl, Sandra, aren't you. Pretty as they come. There was – let me see, who was it? – Susie, last week. That's right, Susie." Her eyes investigated, quick as mice. "Put your jacket on the back of the door, dear, you won't want to get that messy. Still at school, are you?"

The boy said "I'm leaving, July. They're taking me on at the garage, the Blue Star. I been helping out there on and off, before."

Mrs Rutter's smiles folded into one another. Above them, her eyes examined him. "Well, I expect that's good steady money if you'd nothing special in mind. Sugar?"

There was a view from the window out over a bedraggled

garden with the stumps of spent vegetables and a matted flowerbed and a square of shaggy grass. Beyond, the spinney reached up to the fence, a no-man's-land of willowherb and thistle and small trees, growing thicker and higher into the full density of woodland. Mrs Rutter said, "Yes, you have a look out, aren't I lucky – right up beside the wood. Lovely it is in the spring, the primroses and that. Mind, there's not as many as there used to be."

The girl said, "Have you lived here for a long time?"

"Most of my life, dear. I came here as a young married woman, and that's a long way back, I can tell you. You'll be courting before long yourself, I don't doubt. Like bees round the honeypot, they'll be."

The girl blushed. She looked at the floor, at her own feet, neat and slim and brown. She touched, secretly, the soft skin of her thigh; she felt her breasts poke up and out at the thin stuff of her top; she licked the inside of her teeth, that had only the one filling, a speck like a pin-head. She wished there was Susie to have a giggle with, not just Kerry Stevens.

The boy said, "What'd you like us to do?"

His chin was explosive with acne; at his middle, his jeans yawned from his T-shirt, showing pale chilly flesh. Mrs Rutter said, "I expect you're a nice strong boy, aren't you? I daresay you'd like to have a go at the grass with the old mower. Sandra can give this room a do, that would be nice, it's as much as I can manage to have a dust of the ornaments just now, I can't get down to the floor."

When he had gone outside the girl fetched broom and mop and dustpan from a cupboard under the narrow stair. The cupboard, stacked with yellowing newspapers, smelt of damp and mouse. When she returned the old woman was back in the armchair, a composite chintzy mass from which cushions oozed and her voice flowed softly on. "That's it, dear, you just work round, give the corners a brush if you don't mind, that's where the dust settles. Mind your pretty skirt, pull it up a bit, there's only me to see if you're showing a bit of bum. That's ever such a nice style, I expect your mum made it, did she?"

The girl said, "Actually I did."

"Well now, fancy! You're a little dressmaker, too, are you? I was good with my needle when I was younger, my eyesight's past it now, of course. I made my own wedding-dress, ivory silk with lace insets. A *Vogue* pattern it was, with a sweetheart neckline."

The door opened. Kerry said, "Where'll I put the clippings?"

"There's the compost heap down the bottom, by the fence. And while you're down there could you get some sticks from the wood for kindling, there's a good lad."

When he had gone she went on, "That's a nice boy. It's a pity they put that stuff on their hair these days, sticky-looking. I expect you've got lots of boyfriends, though, haven't you?"

The girl poked in a crack at a clump of fluff. "I don't really know Kerry that much."

"Don't you, dear. Well, I expect you get all sorts, in your club thing, the club that Miss Hammond runs."

"The Good Neighbours. Pat, we call her."

"She was down here last week. Ever such a nice person. Kind. It's sad she never married."

The girl said, "Is that your husband in the photo, Mrs Rutter?"

"That's right, dear. In his uniform. The Ox and Bucks. After he got his stripes. He was a lovely man."

She sat back on her heels, the dustpan on her lap. The photo was yellowish, in a silver frame. "Did he . . . ?"

"Killed in the war, dear. Right at the start. He was in one

of the first campaigns, in Belgium, and he never came back."

The girl saw a man with a tooth-brush moustache, his army cap slicing his forehead. "That's terrible."

"Tragic. There was a lot of tragedies in the war. It's nice it won't be like that for you young people nowadays. Touch wood, cross fingers. I like young people, I never had any children, it's been a loss, that, I've got a sympathy with young people."

The girl emptied the dustpan into the bin outside the back door. Beyond the fence, she could see the bushes thrash and Kerry's head bob among them. She thought, rather him than me, but it's different for boys, for him anyway, he's not a nervy type, it's if you're nervy you get bothered about things like Packer's End.

She was nervy, she knew. Mum always said so.

Mrs Rutter was rummaging in a cupboard by her chair. "Chocky? I always keep a few chockies by for visitors." She brought out a flowered tin. "There. Do you know, I've had this twenty years, all but. Look at the little cornflowers. And the daisies. They're almost real, aren't they?"

"Sweet," said the girl.

"Take them out and see if what's-'is-name would like one?"

There was a cindery path down the garden, ending at a compost heap where eggshells gleamed among leaves and grassclippings. Rags of plastic fluttered from sticks in a bed of cabbages. The girl picked her way daintily, her toes wincing against the cinders. A place in the country. One day she would have a place in the country, but not like this. Sometime. A little white house peeping over a hill, with a stream at the bottom of a crisp green lawn and an orchard with old apple trees and a brown pony. And she would walk in the long grass in this orchard in a straw hat with these two children, a boy and a girl, children with fair shiny hair like hers, and there'd be this man.

She leaned over the fence and shouted, "Hey . . ."

"What?"

She brandished the box.

He came up, dumping an armful of sticks. "What's this for, then?"

"She said. Help yourself."

He fished among the sweets, his fingers etched with dirt. "I did a job on your dad's car last week. That blue Escort's his, isn't it?"

"Mmn."

"July, I'll be starting full-time. When old Bill retires. With day-release at the tech."

She thought of oily workshop floors, of the foetid undersides of cars. She couldn't stand the feel of dirt, if her hands were the least bit grubby she had to go and wash, a rim of grime under her nails could make her shudder. She said, "I don't know how you can, all that muck."

He fished for another chocolate. "Nothing wrong with a bit of dirt. What you going to do, then?"

"Secretarial."

Men didn't mind so much. At home, her dad did things like unblocking the sink and cleaning the stove; mum was the same as her, just the feel of grease and stuff made her squirm. They couldn't either of them wear anything that had a stain or a spot.

He said "I don't go much on her."

"Who?"

He waved towards the cottage.

"She's all right. What's wrong with her, then?"

He shrugged. "I dunno. The way she talks and that."

"She lost her husband," said the girl. "In the war." She

considered him, across the fence, over a chasm. Mum said boys matured later, in many ways.

"There's lots of people done that."

She looked beyond him, into distances. "Tragic, actually. Well, I'll go back and get on. She says can you see to her bins when you've got the sticks. She wants them carried down for the dustmen."

Mrs Rutter watched her come in, glinting from the cushions. "That's a good girl. Put the tin back in the cupboard, dear."

"What would you like me to do now?"

"There's my little bit of washing by the sink. Just the personal things to rinse through. That would be ever so kind."

The girl ran water into the basin. She measured in the soapflakes. She squeezed the pastel nylons, the floating sinuous tights. "It's a lovely colour, that turquoise."

"My niece got me that last Christmas. Nightie and a little jacket to go. I was telling you about my wedding dress. The material came from Macy's, eight yards. I cut it on the cross, for the hang. Of course, I had a figure then." She heaved herself round in the chair. "You're a lovely shape, Sandra. You take care you stay that way."

"I can get a spare tyre," the girl said. "If I'm not careful."

Outside, the bin lids rattled.

"I hope he's minding my edging. I've got lobelia planted out along that path."

"I love blue flowers."

"You should see the wood in the spring, with the bluebells. There's a place right far in where you get lots coming up still. I used to go in there picking every year before my leg started playing me up. Jugs and jugs of them, for the scent. Haven't you ever seen them?"

The girl shook her head. She wrung out the clothes,

gathered up the damp skein. "I'll put these on the line, shall I?"

When she returned the boy was bringing in the filled coal-scuttle and a bundle of sticks.

"That's it" said Mrs Rutter. "Under the sink, that's where they go. You'll want to have a wash after that, won't you. Put the kettle on, Sandra, and we'll top up the pot."

The boy ran his hands under the tap. His shirt clung to his shoulder-blades, damp with sweat. He looked over the bottles of detergent, the jug of parsley, the handful of flowers tucked into a coronation mug. He said, "Is that the wood where there was that German plane came down in the war?"

"Don't start on that," said the girl. "It gives me the willies."

"What for?"

"Scary."

The old woman reached forward and prodded the fire. "Put a bit of coal on for me, there's a good boy. What's to be scared of? It's over and done with, good riddance to bad rubbish."

"It was there, then?"

"Shut up," said the girl.

"Were you here?"

"Fill my cup up, dear, would you. I was here. Me and my sister. My sister Dot. She's dead now, two years. Heart. That was before she was married, of course, nineteen forty-two, it was."

"Did you see it come down?"

She chuckled. "I saw it come down all right."

"What was it?" said the boy "Messerschmitt?"

"How would I know that, dear? I don't know anything about aeroplanes. Anyway, it was all smashed up by the time I saw it, you couldn't have told t'other from which."

The girl's hand hovered, the tea-cup halfway to her mouth. She sipped, put it down. "You *saw* it? Ooh, I wouldn't have gone anywhere near."

"It would have been burning," said the boy. "It'd have gone up in flames."

"There weren't any flames, it was just stuck there in the ground, end up, with mess everywhere. Drop more milk, dear, if you don't mind."

The girl shuddered. "I s'pose they'd taken the bodies away by then."

Mrs Rutter picked out a tea-leaf with the tip of the spoon. She drank, patted the corner of her mouth delicately with a tissue. "No, no, 'course not. There was no one else seen it come down. We'd heard the engine and you could tell there was trouble, the noise wasn't right, and we looked out and saw it come down smack in the trees. 'Course we hadn't the telephone so there was no ringing the police or the Warden at Clapton. Dot said we should maybe bike to the village but it was a filthy wet night, pouring cats and dogs, and fog too, and we didn't know if it was one of ours or one of theirs, did we? So Dot said better go and have a look first."

"But either way . . ." the boy began.

"We got our wellies on, and Dot had the big lantern, and we went off. It wasn't very far in. We found it quite quick and Dot grabbed hold of me and pointed and we saw one of the wings sticking up with the markings on and we knew it was one of theirs. We cheered, I can tell you."

The boy stared at her over the rim of the cup, blank-faced.

"Dot said bang goes some more of the bastards, come on let's get back into the warm and we just started back when we heard this noise."

"Noise?"

"Sort of moaning."

"Oh," cried the girl. "How awful, weren't they . . ."

"So we got up closer and Dot held the lantern so we could see and there was three of them, two in the front and they was dead, you could see that all right, one of them had his . . ."

The girl grimaced. "Don't."

Mrs Rutter's chins shook, the pink and creamy chins. "Good job you weren't there, then, my duck. Not that we were laughing at the time, I can tell you, rain teaming down and a raw November night, and that sight under our noses. It wasn't pretty but I've never been squeamish, nor Dot neither. And then we saw the other one."

"The other one?" said the boy warily.

"The one at the back. He was trapped, see, the way the plane had broken up. There wasn't any way he could get out."

The girl stiffened. "Oh, lor, you mean he . . ."

"He was hurt pretty bad. He was kind of talking to himself. Something about mutter, mutter . . . Dot said he's not going to last long, and a good job too, three of them that'll be. She'd been a V.A.D. so she knew a bit about casualties, see." Mrs Rutter licked her lips; she looked across at them, her eyes darting. "Then we went back to the cottage."

There was silence. The fire gave a heave and a sigh. "You what?" said the boy.

"Went back inside. It was bucketing down, cats and dogs."

The boy and girl sat quite still, on the far side of the table.

"That was eighteen months or so after my hubby didn't come back from Belgium." Her eyes were on the girl; the girl looked away. "Tit for tat, I said to Dot."

After a moment she went on. "Next morning it was still raining and blow me if the bike hadn't got a puncture. I said

49

to Dot I'm not walking to the village in this, and that's flat, and Dot was running a bit of a temp, she had the 'flu or something coming on. I tucked her up warm and when I'd done the chores I went back in the wood, to have another look. He must have been a tough so-and-so, that Jerry, he was still mumbling away. It gave me a turn, I can tell you, I'd never imagined he'd last the night. I could see him better, in the day-time; he was bashed up pretty nasty. I'd thought he was an old bloke, too, but he wasn't. He'd have been twentyish, that sort of age."

The boy's spoon clattered to the floor; he did not move.

"I reckon he may have seen me, not that he was in a state to take much in. He called out something. I thought, oh no, you had this coming to you, mate, there's a war on. You won't know that expression – it was what everybody said in those days. I thought, why should I do anything for you? Nobody did anything for my Bill, did they? I was a widow at thirty-nine. I've been on my own ever since."

The boy shoved his chair back from the table.

"He must have been a tough bastard, like I said. He was still there that evening, but the next morning he was dead. The weather'd perked up by then and I walked to the village and got a message to the people at Clapton. They were ever so surprised; they didn't know there'd been a Jerry plane come down in the area at all. There were lots of people came to take bits for souvenirs, I had a bit myself but it's got mislaid, you tend to mislay things when you get to my age."

The boy had got up. He glanced down at the girl. "I'm going," he said. "Dunno about you, but I'm going."

She stared at the lacy cloth on the table, the fluted china cup. "I'll come too."

"Eh?" said the old woman. "You're off, are you? That was nice of you to see to my little jobs for me. Tell what's-'er-name to send someone next week if she can, I like having someone young about the place, once in a while, I've got a sympathy with young people. Here – you're forgetting your pretty jacket, Sandra, what's the hurry? 'Bye then, my ducks, see you close my gate, won't you?"

The boy walked ahead, fast; the girl pattered behind him, sliding on the dry grass. At the gateway into the cornfield he stopped. He said, not looking at her, looking towards the furzy edge of the wood, "Christ!"

The wood sat there in the afternoon sun. Wind stirred the trees. Birds sang. There were not, the girl realised, wolves or witches or tigers. Nor were there prowling blokes, gypsy type blokes. And there were not chattering ghostly voices. Somewhere there were some scraps of metal overlooked by people hunting for souvenirs.

The boy said, "I'm not going near that old bitch again." He leaned against the gate, clenching his fists on an iron rung; he shook slightly. "I won't ever forget him, that poor sod."

She nodded.

"Two bloody nights. Christ!"

And she would hear, she thought, always, for a long time anyway, that voice trickling on, that soft old woman's voice; would see a tin painted with cornflowers, pretty china ornaments.

"It makes you want to throw up," he said. "Someone like that."

She couldn't think of anything to say. He had grown; he had got older and larger. His anger eclipsed his acne, the patches of grease on his jeans, and lardy midriff. You could get people all wrong, she realised with alarm. You could get people wrong and there was a darkness that was not the darkness of tree shadows and murky undergrowth and you could not draw the curtains and keep it out because it was in

51

your head, once known, in your head for ever like lines from a song. One moment you were walking in long grass with the sun on your hair and birds singing and the next you glimpsed darkness, an inescapable darkness. The darkness was out there and it was a part of you and you would never be without it, ever.

She walked behind him, through a world grown unreliable, in which flowers sparkle and birds sing but everything is not as it appears, oh no.

The pill-box

THE WRITER OF a story has an infinity of choices. An infinity of narratives; an infinity of endings. The process of choosing, of picking this set of events rather than that, of ending up here rather than there – well, call it what you like: craft, art, accident, intuition.

Call it what you like, it's a curious process.

I teach Eng. Lit. Consequently I try to point this sort of thing out to the young. Life and literature – all that. Parallels; illuminations. I'm no mystic, but there's one thing that never ceases to astonish me: the fixity of things. That we live with it, accept it as we do. That we do not question that the course of events is thus, and never could be other. When you think of how nearly, at every moment, it is not.

Think of it. Stare it in the face and think of it.

I come out of my front gate, I bump into old Sanders next door, we have a chat . . . Shift the point at which I emerge by ever so little, and I do not meet Sanders, we do not have a word about the cricket club dinner, he does not offer to drop over later with his Black & Decker and fix that shelf for me.

I cross the street, looking first to right and left, a lorry passes, I alight upon the pavement opposite.

I cross the street, not looking first to right and left; the

53

lorry driver's concentration lapses for a second, I am so much meat under his wheels.

Some bloke is gunned down in Sarajevo. In another country, evil is bred. And then and then and then . . . A tired voice comes from a crackling wireless: there is war. "May God bless you all," he says.

A trigger jams. Elsewhere, a mad house-painter dies young of polio. And then, and then, and then . . . 3rd September 1939 is a fine day, sunshine with a hint of showers.

Oh well *of course* you say, any fool can play those games. Intriguing but unproductive. We inhabit, after all, a definite world; facts are facts. The sequence of my life, of your life, of the public life.

Listen, then. I went up to the pill-box this evening – the wartime pill-box on the top.

The pill-box is on the brow of the hill and faces square down the lane. I take my time getting up there; it's a steep pull up and the outlook's half the point of the walk. I have a rest at the first gate, and then at the end by the oak, and again at the gate to Clapper's field. You get the view from there: the village down below you and the fields reaching away to the coast and the sea hanging at the edge of the green, a long grey smear with maybe a ship or two and on clear days the white glimmer of the steelworks over on the Welsh coast.

It was sited to cover anything coming up and heading on over the hill. Heading for the main road – that would have been the idea, I suppose. It would have had the village covered, too, and a good part of the valley. Very small it looks now, stuck there at the edge of the field: barely room for a couple of blokes inside. I never know why it's not been taken away – much longer and it'll be a historical monument I daresay and they'll slap a protection order on it. The field is rough grazing and always has been so I suppose no one's felt any great call to get rid of it. Dalton's field, it is; from time to time you find he's stashed some cattle feed away in the pill-box, or a few bags of lime. It comes in handy for the village lads, too, always has done: get your girl up there, nice bit of shelter . . . I've made use of it that way myself in my time. Back in – oh, forty-seven or thereabouts. Yes, forty-seven, that spring it rained cats and dogs and there was flooding right left and centre. Rosie Parks, black curly hair and an answer to everything. Lying in there with the rain coming down in spears outside; "You lay off, Keith Harrison, I'm telling you . . .", "Ah, come on, Rosie . . .", Giggle giggle.

The rain started this evening when I was at the oak, just a sprinkle, and by the time I got to the top it was coming down hard and looked set in for a while so I ducked down into the pill-box to sit it out.

I was thinking about the past, in a vague kind of way – the war, being young. Looking out from inside the pill-box you see the countryside as a bright green rectangle, very clear, lots of detail, like a photo. And I've got good eyesight anyway, even at fifty-seven, just about a hundred per cent vision. I could see the new houses they've put up on the edge of the village and I was thinking that the place has changed a lot since I was a boy, and yet in other ways it hasn't. The new estate, the shop, cars at every door, telly aerials, main drainage; but the same names, by and large, same families, same taste to the beer, same stink from Clapper's silage in hot weather.

I can see the house where I was born, from the pill-box. And the one I live in now. The churchyard, where my parents are, God bless 'em. The recreation ground beside the church hall where we used to drill in 1941; those of us left behind, too old like Jim Blockley at sixty-odd, too young like me at seventeen-and-a-half, too wonky like the postmaster with his bronchitis, too valuable like the farmers and the doctor.

I can see the road, too – the road that takes me daily to work. Ten miles to Scarhead to try to drum a bit of sense and a bit of knowledge into forty fifteen-year-old heads. Full cycle. Back then, mine was the empty head, the bloke at the blackboard was . . . was old Jenkins, Jenks. It's not been a mistake, coming back. I'd always thought I'd like to. The day I saw the advert. in the *Times Ed. Supp.* I knew at once I'd apply. Yes, I thought, that's it, that's for me, end up back at home, why not? I've always thought of it as home, down here, wherever I've been – Nottingham, up on the north-east, London. Not that it's local boy made good, exactly. Teaching's a tidy enough occupation, they reckon down here, but not high-flying. Farmers do a sight better. I don't drive a Jag, like Tim Matlock who was in my class at the grammar and farms up on the county border now. Not that I care tuppence.

I lit a pipe to keep the midges off; the rain was coming down harder than ever. It looked as though I might have to pack in the rest of my walk. I opened the newspaper: usual stuff, miners reject pay offer, Middle East talks, rail fares up.

When I heard the first voice I thought there was someone outside in the field – some trick of the acoustics, making it sound as though it were in the pill-box.

"They're bloody coming!" he said.

And then another bloke, a young one, a boy, gave a sort of grunt. You knew, somehow, he was on edge. His voice had that crack to it, that pitch of someone who's keyed up, holding himself in. Shit-scared.

"Can I have a look, Mr Barnes? Oh God – I see them. Heading straight up."

How can I put it? Describe how it was. The words that come to mind are banal, clichés: eery, unearthly, uncanny.

They were there, but they were not. They were in the head, but yet were outside it. There were two men, an old and a younger, who spoke from some other dimension; who were there with me in the pill-box and yet also were not, could not be, had never been.

Listen again.

"Give me them field-glasses . . . They've set Clapper's barn on fire. There's more tanks on the Scarhead road – six, seven . . . They'll be at the corner in a few minutes now, son."

And the young chap speaks again. "O.K." he says. "O.K., I'm ready."

The voices, you understand, are overlaid by other noises, ordinary noises: the rain on the roof of the pill-box, sheep, a tractor in the lane. The tractor goes past but the voices don't take a blind bit of notice. The old bloke tells the other one to pass him another clip of ammo. "You all right, son?" he says, the boy answers that is he all right. There is that high sharp note in his voice, in both their voices.

There is a silence.

And then they come back.

"I can see him now. Armoured car. Two."

"O.K. Yes. I've got them."

"Hold it. Hold it, son . . ."

"Yes. Right . . ."

"Hold it. Steady. When they get to the oak."

"O.K., Mr Barnes."

And everything is quiet again. A quiet you could cut with a knife. The inside of the pill-box is tight-strung, waiting; it is both a moment in time and a time that is going on for ever, will go on for ever. I drop my tobacco tin and it clatters on the concrete floor but the sound does not break that other quiet, which, I now realise, is somewhere else, is something else.

57

The old bloke says, "Fire!"

And then they are both talking together. There is no other sound, nothing, just their voices. And the rain.

The boy says, "I got him, my God, I got him!" and the other one says, "Steady. Re-load now. Steady. Wait till the second one's moving again. Right. Fire!"

"We hit him!"

"He's coming on . . ."

"Christ there's another behind!"

"Bastards! Jerry bastards!"

And the boy cries, "That's for my dad! And that's for my mum! Come on then, bloody come on then . . ."

"Steady, son. Hold it a minute, there's a . . ."

"What's he doing, Christ he's . . ."

"He's got a grenade. Keep on firing, for God's sake. Keep him covered."

And suddenly they go quiet. Quite quiet. Except that just once the old bloke says something. He says, "Don't move, Keith, keep still, I'm coming over, I . . ."

He says, "Keith?"

And there is nothing more.

I went on sitting there. The quietness left the inside of the pill-box, that other quietness. The tractor came back down the lane again. The rain stopped. A blackbird started up on the roof of the pill-box. Down in the valley there was a patch of sunlight slap on the village; the church very bright, a car windscreen flashing, pale green of the chestnuts in the pub car park.

I knew, now, that from the first moment there'd been something about that young chap's voice. The boy.

Mr Barnes. Joe Barnes worked the manor farm in the war. He left here sometime ago, retired to Ilfracombe; he died a year or two back.

I was in his platoon, in 1941. I've not thought of him in

years. Couldn't put a face to him, now. He died of cancer in
a nursing-home in Ilfracombe. Didn't he?

Or.

Or he died in a pill-box up on the hill above the village,
long ago. Him and a boy called Keith. In which case the
pill-box is no longer there nor I take it the village nor the
whole bloody place at least not in any way you or I could
know it.

No young fellow called Keith ever put his hand up the
skirt of Rosie Parks in that pill-box, nor did another bloke, a
fifty-seven year old teacher of English, walk up that way of
an evening for a smoke and a look at the view.

I came out, filled my pipe, looked down at the village. All
right, yes, I thought to myself – interesting, the imaginative
process. The mind churning away, putting pictures to a line
of thought. I dozed off in there.

Later I knew I did not imagine it. I heard it. Heard them.
So what do you make of that? Eh? What can anyone make of
it? How, having glimpsed the possibility of the impossible,
can the world remain as steady as you had supposed?

Suppose that the writer of a story were haunted, in the
mind, for ever, by all those discarded alternatives, by the
voices of all those assorted characters. Forced to preserve
them always as the price of creative choice.

Then suppose, by the same token, that just once in a
while it is given to any one of us to experience the inconceivable. To push through the barrier of what we know into
the heady breathtaking unbearable ozone of what we cannot
contemplate. Did that happen to me? In the pill-box on the
hill on a summer Monday evening, with the world steady
under my feet and the newspaper in my hand, telling me
what's what, how the world is, where we are?

Customers

MAJOR ANGLESEY AND Mrs Yardley-Peters worked slowly up and down the aisles of the chain store. They picked up garments and held them against each other. Mrs Yardley-Peters undid her coat, and Major Anglesey tried blouses around the broad slope of her bosom, measuring them carefully armpit to armpit. Mrs Yardley-Peters pondered over a red paisley dressing-gown, chest forty, looking from the pattern to the Major's rather ruddy complexion and gingery toothbrush moustache. Rejecting the blouses and the dressing-gown, they paused at the hosiery counter, where Mrs Yardley-Peters selected three pairs of tights (Brown Haze, Large) and paid for them at the nearest cash desk. They hesitated for a long while over ladies' v-neck lambswool sweaters, eventually deciding on a light grey size sixteen which Mrs Yardley-Peters popped into her shopping bag.

At Men's Accessories, Major Anglesey held various ties under his chin and decided on a red and navy stripe, which he folded tidily and put in his pocket. From there they wandered to the shoe section. Major Anglesey tried on a pair of brown brogues, took a step or two and shook his head, returning them to the rack. Mrs Yardley-Peters, meanwhile, had put on some black pumps – size four since, although a stout woman and not short, she had surprisingly

61

small feet. The Major nodded approval and Mrs Yardley-Peters slipped her own shoes into the shopping bag, keeping on the pumps. Major Anglesey, at this point, glanced at his watch, said something, and the two of them moved rather more quickly to the food department where they filled a wire basket with a carton of coleslaw, two portions of cooked chicken, a packet of jam fancies and a jar of powdered coffee, lining up with those at the checkout.

The store detective, having joined them at the time of the red and navy striped tie, stood discreetly to one side. She was an unexceptional-looking woman, wearing a brown crimplene dress and fawn anorak, with a basket over one arm. The basket held, today, a bunch of bananas and a packet of Kleenex. She tended to vary the contents; meat, of course, would not do, being inclined to go bad in the heat of the store, over a long day.

Major Anglesey and Mrs Yardley-Peters passed through the checkout and back into the main part of the shop. At the entrance, they stopped for a moment, Mrs Yardley-Peters being evidently fussed in case she had lost her gloves; a search of her handbag, however, apparently put things right, and they proceeded under the blast of tropical wind issuing from somewhere in the ceiling and out into the street.

The store detective caught up with them at the zebra crossing, as they stood waiting for a lull in the traffic. She asked if they would please come back to the manager's office. The Major and Mrs Yardley-Peters received this request with considerable surprise but made no objection, except that the Major looked again at his watch and said he hoped it wouldn't take too long, as it was getting on for lunch-time.

Several sales assistants, watching the detective walk through the store a step or two behind Major Anglesey and Mrs Yardley-Peters, exchanged glances and grinned. One girl stuck her chest out and mimicked the store detective's slightly military gait; it was a standing joke that Madge, having made a capture, went all official. At that point, the crimplene dress and the anorak took on, if you knew what you were looking at, the authority of the uniform she would herself have much preferred and that she had so regretted when giving up the traffic-warden job. In most other respects, of course, her present position was far preferable. Her friends occasionally said that they didn't know how she could do a job like that, going on to add, uncertainly, that of course they supposed someone had to . . . Personally, she never found it a problem; people could be a lot more unpleasant when you handed them a parking ticket. Aggressive. Your average shop-lifter tended to crumple; she'd hardly ever – bar a gang of French schoolchildren once – had any trouble. And it was a sight warmer, on a winter afternoon, than patrolling the windy lengths of the High Street.

The manager, seated behind his desk, listened in silence to the store detective's account of the events of the last half hour. So, at first, did Mrs Yardley-Peters and Major Anglesey, until the Major began to shake his head, more in sorrow than distress, it seemed, and Mrs Yardley-Peters exclaimed, "Oh, gracious me, no," and then, "No, no, it wasn't like that at all, you see we . . ." The store detective continued her account, as unemphasized as recitative.

The manager said to Mrs Yardley-Peters, "Would you open your shopping-bag, please?"

At first Mrs Yardley-Peters did not appear to take this in. She was rummaging again in her handbag. After a moment she said, "Ah, *there* it is." And then, "Oh no, I'd rather not, really, you see I've got it all sorted out, with the squashy things on top."

The manager turned to Major Anglesey. "It would really be much better if your wife . . ."

The Major made a small gesture. "The lady," he said with dignity, "is my mistress."

Mrs Yardley-Peters patted her hair, which was greying and set in neat ridges, a style that somehow disturbed the manager – it reminded him of something and he could not think what. "That's right. Until my divorce comes through, you understand. Which should be before Christmas all being well but you know what lawyers are. They drag their feet so. Have you ever had dealings with lawyers, Mr er . . . ?"

The manager swallowed. The store detective, who was standing beside the desk as though at attention, shifted position and drew in breath with a little hiss.

Mrs Yardley-Peters glanced round the room and located a chair. "I must sit down for a minute. I've got this trouble with swollen ankles, and in any case . . ." – She looked down at the black pumps, frowning – "You know, I've a horrid feeling I should have had a half size larger. These are pinching."

The manager said, "Can you show me a receipt for those shoes, madam?"

"Receipt?" Mrs Yardley-Peters appeared bewildered. "Oh, from the place where you pay . . . Well, no, in fact I don't remember . . . I expect the Major paid, did you, dear? But you know I think I'll have to change them." She turned to the store detective. "Do you do half sizes – I didn't notice. A four-and-a-half, it would need to be."

The manager remembered suddenly that Mrs Yardley-Peters' hairstyle reminded him of the actress who played the Duchess of Windsor in that TV series, though of course she was dark and much younger. This small satisfaction went some way to halt his mounting sense of disorientation. He said, "I must ask you again to open your shopping-bag, madam."

"Oh, I say" said Major Anglesey.

Mrs Yardley-Peters looked at the manager in bewilderment. "I do think . . ." she began, and then, "Oh well, I suppose if I'm careful." She lifted out the packaged jam fancies and the chicken pieces. The store detective swayed forward, peering into the bag; "That's the sweater, and that's her own shoes."

"That's right," said Mrs Yardley-Peters. "You know, I wonder if I won't put them back on." She was stacking things on the manager's desk.

The store detective straightened. She had gone quite red in the face. Her stomach rumbled.

The manager turned to Major Anglesey. "May I please see the tie that you put in your pocket."

The Major blinked. "Tie? Oh, yes – rather." He took out the tie and laid it on the desk.

"I'm not sure about that red, after all," said Mrs Yardley-Peters. The store detective's stomach rumbled again. Mrs Yardley-Peters opened her handbag. "I should have a magnesia tablet somewhere. Yes, here we are." The store detective took a step backwards, violently, and landed against the wall of the office, as though at bay. "No?" said Mrs Yardley-Peters, "I always find they do the trick. It's getting near your lunch-time, I expect." She eased off the black shoes, grimacing.

The manager realised he was losing his grip; tears he could cope with, protestations of innocence, truculence. He said, "You understand that unless you can provide some proof that you paid for these goods I shall have to call the police?"

"Oh, I say," said Major Anglesey again. Mrs Yardley-Peters, now in stockinged feet, flexed her toes; "Oh, my goodness, I shouldn't do that, specially since it's all a silly mistake. You get into the most frightfully deep waters once you're involved with the police. My husband and I – my ex-husband, that is, all but – had an awful business once after we were the only people who saw this road accident. Witnesses, you see. Oh no – I don't think you should involve the police, not that they can't be awfully efficient sometimes, I will say that."

The manager lined up the papers on his desk, for something to occupy the hands, and looked steadily at Major Anglesey; it was better, he found, though better wasn't really the word under the circumstances, if he simply tried to pretend the woman wasn't there. The store detective made a strangled noise. The manager said, rather sharply, "Yes, all *right*, Mrs Hebden. Now, sir, did you pay for that tie, and did your – did the lady pay for the sweater and the shoes?"

"Oh, I don't think so," said Major Anglesey. "No, I don't think she would have. You see, it was a question of whether she'd left her cheque book in the car or whether . . ."

"I've got it, Rupert," said Mrs Yardley-Peters. "It's quite all right – it was in my bag all along, isn't that silly."

The Major patted her shoulder. "But at the time there was this bother about whether it was lost or not, so if anyone paid it would have been me. No doubt about that."

"He didn't," said the store detective.

"Really?" said Major Anglesey. "Well, that's an extraordinary thing." He looked at the tie. "One wouldn't have bothered with a cheque for that, of course, it can't have cost more than a pound or two."

"You should have had the blue one," said Mrs Yardley-Peters. "That's not going to be any good with your dark suit, you know."

The manager made a convulsive movement and shot a black plastic pen container onto the floor. Major Anglesey,

66

with cries of concern, got down and scrabbled for the pens –
"Here we are, all intact, I think."

"So silly," said Mrs Yardley-Peters, "about the cheque
book. Shall I pay you back while it's in my head, Rupert. I'll
write *you* a cheque."

"Look," said the manager, with a sort of gasp, "I simply
want to . . ."

"Consider them a present my dear," said the Major
gallantly.

"You didn't pay for them," said the store detective. The
words came out as a hoarse cry and both the Major and Mrs
Yardley-Peters turned to look at her in surprise. Mrs Yardley-
Peters shook her head and frowned, evidently put out, "No,
no, that's absurd. You've just heard the Major say they're to
be counted as a present and that's sweet of you, Rupert,
though I do think we ought to keep our finances separate at
least for the time being. You know, I'm wondering if the
shoes may not be all right once one's worn them in a bit.
Do you usually reckon," she went on, addressing the store
detective, "on them giving a bit as you wear them?"

"Mrs Hebden is not a member of the sales staff," said the
manager. "And in any case it is hardly a question of . . ."

The Major interrupted. "I remember now, it all comes
back – that tie was one pound ninety-five. I thought at the
time good grief in real money that's all of two quid and I've
got ties in my cupboard I paid four-and-six for, in the old
days. Two quid for a tie, I ask you! Not," he went on
quickly, "that it's not good value for nowadays."

The manager rose. His collar clung to his neck and sweat
trickled down inside his shirt. He went to the window and
opened it.

"Yes, I was feeling it was a wee bit stuffy too," said Mrs
Yardley-Peters. "You'd think they'd give you a bigger
office, wouldn't you? But I suppose you're out and about

quite a lot, looking after the shop. I always say, the thing about this sort of place is, you can see exactly what you're getting, and there's never a bit of argument about changing anything."

Once, the manager had had to deal with an Arab lady and her three daughters, not a word of English between them, all weeping, and twenty-eight pairs of bikini briefs stuffed inside their coats. At this moment, he looked back on that occasion almost with nostalgia. He sat down again and addressed the Major. "Now, sir, if there is any explanation you feel you'd like to give, naturally I . . ."

The note of hysteria in his voice did not escape Mrs Yardley-Peters. She said kindly, "You know you look to me a bit under the weather, I should think you might be coming down with something. If I were you I'd . . ."

The Major tapped her reprovingly. "Mona, I'm sure our friend here's well able to take care of himself. All he wants is to get this bit of bother sorted out so we can all be off for our dins."

Madge Hebden, all her life, had had strong feelings about legality. She'd never, herself, stepped out of line, not once. And she believed in plain speaking. At this point she exploded.

"It's theft, that's what it is! Honest to goodness theft. Thieves! Bit of bother, indeed! I saw them with my own eyes and in all the ten months I've been in the store I've never . . ."

The manager got to his feet in one violent movement. His hands, as though acting independently of the rest of him, twitched about the surface of the desk, apparently seeking a hold on something. "Thank you, Mrs Hebden, you've done a grand job. In this case I feel though that there may be extenuating circumstances to be taken into consideration" – he was gabbling now, looking through and beyond rather than at Major Anglesey and Mrs Yardley-Peters – "and naturally one prefers rather than perpetrate possibly an injustice to exercise in some cases and I believe this to be one such discretion as is at one's disposal our policy in such instances being always to . . ."

"Oh dear," said Mrs Yardley-Peters, "I'm afraid I'm not following this very well. Could you begin again."

The manager wiped his forehead. He said, "Go away."

"Eh?" said the Major.

"Please go. Just go."

Mrs Yardley-Peters stared at him. "Well, I must say. I think that's a bit abrupt. After all, you invited us in here, it wasn't us who wanted to come. Very well, then." She bent down and put her shoes on. The manager, leaning across the desk, pushed towards her the contents of the shopping bag. Mrs Yardley-Peters put them carefully into it, slowly, removing things once or twice to re-arrange them. As she picked up the shoes, the lambswool sweater and the tie the store detective gave a kind of croak; the manager was silent, nerves twitching all over one side of his face.

"There," said Mrs Yardley-Peters. She rose. "Have you got the car-keys, Rupert, or have I?" At the door she paused and looked back. "You know one doesn't like to interfere but I do have the most distinct impression that they over-work you people, the powers that be. You both look done in."

Major Anglesey and Mrs Yardley-Peters walked slowly through the shop. Mid-way they paused and Major Anglesey took over the shopping bag. They stopped once to cast an eye over the shirt counter but evidently decided against any further acquisitions. At the entrance Major Anglesey held the door open for a woman with a push-chair and was then trapped for a couple of minutes by his own solicitude, as a procession of people entered from the street;

at last he was able to join Mrs Yardley-Peters outside and the two of them moved away towards the multi-storey car park.

Major Anglesey drove. Mrs Yardley-Peters remarked that that poor man had seemed awfully neurotic, and the assistant rather bad-tempered. Detective, Mona, corrected the Major, they call them detective. Whatever they are, said Mrs Yardley-Peters, anyway, it's not a job I'd care for. The Major agreed. They recalled one or two previous experiences. When they reached the bungalow the Major put the car in the garage and carried the shopping bag inside. Mrs Yardley-Peters, humming to herself, removed the food items; the Major took the bag into the spare bedroom. He put the lambswool sweater, still in its plastic wrapping, into a big cupboard whose shelves were filled with many other sweaters, cardigans, shirts and pajamas, also still in their wrappings. The tie he added to a rail already piled with ties, in a wardrobe pressed tight with suits and coats and ladies' dresses, from which dangled price tickets and labels giving washing instructions. Mrs Yardley-Peters came in and said playfully, "Have I been a clever girl?"; the Major, without speaking, patted her bottom. "Din-dins," said Mrs Yardley-Peters, and the Major followed her through into the sitting-room, where the chicken pieces and the coleslaw were set out on Beatrix Potter plates. "My turn for Jemima Puddleduck," said Mrs Yardley-Peters. The Major poured light ale from a can into glasses decorated with cartoon mice; "Cheers." Mrs Yardley-Peters looked at him roguishly over the top of her glass. "Cheers, Rupie. We've been naughty again, haven't we!" The Major, in reply, waggled his moustache, an accomplishment which had been one of his initial attractions.

Yellow trains

"I AM UNHAPPY," said the girl to her friend. She looked out of the window through the shimmering folds of the net curtains to the parked cars in the street; their windscreens snapped in the sunshine and a small dog rummaged in the gutter. "I am so unhappy," she repeated, and across the city the friend sighed and murmured.

"Yesterday," she said, "I was so happy I could have cried. Listen, I rode in a train with blue seats, bright bright blue, and there was this factory chimney smoking white against the sky and the sky was grey like velvet. Do you know what I mean? And clouds like carvings. I tell you, I sat there looking and I could have cried."

"He isn't," asked the friend delicately, "coming?"

"He isn't coming. There is this business with the office and his mother that he must go to on Saturday come what may and something about someone for whom he has to hold keys to a flat. He isn't coming."

"People," said the friend, after a pause, "get so involved."

The girl watched the small dog nose an empty tin. She looked at the sky above the rooftops and at the thread of vapour from an aeroplane. "I sat in that train and I wasn't thinking of anything in particular. I wasn't thinking:

71

tomorrow, tomorrow, tomorrow. It was just a state of mind. And today . . . Listen, I'm looking at the sky now, and it's nothing. Nothing at all. And yesterday there were these clouds like sculptures. I don't understand how what you see is a question of what you feel."

The friend, across streets and parks and rooftops, sighed again. "Did he phone, or what?"

"He phoned."

"Excuse me a minute," said the friend, "I've got something on the stove."

The girl saw a pigeon with pink twiggy legs walk round and round, round and round. She saw a child go past chanting incantations. She saw an old woman put down a carrier bag and stand for a moment, hunched up.

The friend came back. "Sorry. I expect he just couldn't get out of it."

"Possibly. Probably. I made pizza. And got that beer he likes. He phoned very late last night. I feel as though I've put on pounds and pounds."

"Sorry?" said the friend.

"Weight. Yesterday I felt as though I was floating slightly. Walking along the platform at Clapham Junction. Like bubbles going up through you. And these yellow trains dashing all over the place, yellow like daffodils. I thought, I'm always going to remember feeling like this."

"Mmn."

"And the funny thing is I do now. Remember. I'm miserable, I'm pissed off, I feel as heavy as a rock. But it's all there still, underneath. The floating feeling, and the clouds, and the yellow trains. Only I can't get at it any more."

"Is he going to call again?" asked the friend.

The girl twitched the curtain; the cars shimmered and flashed. "Actually, yesterday I wanted things just to stop

72

there. Until I said go on. I wanted to keep it – feeling like that. I wanted to learn what it was like."

"Looking forward to something," the friend began, "is . . ."

"I wasn't really looking forward. Don't you see? It was just being like that. Happy. Now I'm unhappy and it's nothing, it's a no–feeling. It doesn't exist."

The friend said, "Mmn – I'm not so sure about that." After a moment she added, "I'm sure he'll call again."

"I expect he's calling now," said the girl. "I expect he's desperately trying to get through, dialling and hanging up again and asking the operator if the line's engaged talking or out of order. Dialling and dialling."

The friend coughed. "Excuse me. Where does his mother live?"

"In Surrey. Reigate. His sister lives with her. She has red hair and works in the library. What I can't get over is how things push on like they do and take you with them whether you want it or not. Days. They drag you on. One day you're with the yellow trains like daffodils and the next you're sitting here with a knot in your insides. Sometimes I'm not sure if I can go through with life if this is the way it's going to be."

"Oh, come on now . . ." said the friend. After a moment she went on, "Hello? Are you still there?"

"I'm here. There's this dog outside that's got its paw muddled up in a bit of plastic. Do you think I should go out and help it?"

The friend said, "I don't know. Of course he wouldn't have known about you making the pizza."

"It's all right – the dog's got its paw out of the plastic. I couldn't get the big olives so I had to use the other kind. I had them in my bag when I was walking along the platform at Clapham Junction and now there they are in the fridge.

Same bloody olives. Funny, when you come to think about it."

The friend said sadly, "I suppose you're in love with him."

"Is that my trouble? God, how unoriginal. And here was I going on about clouds and yellow trains. Oh, and there was Battersea Power Station. I didn't tell you about Battersea Power Station. It looked like a temple. Egyptian, I think. Do you imagine he's going to see someone else instead?"

"Look, don't think about that kind of thing."

"I'm not. It's not a question of thinking. I'm not thinking about anything. I just get attacked from time to time."

"I know," said the friend, after a moment.

The girl said, "Do you remember the way when you were a child you always wanted it to be next week? Today was so boring. Next week was always Christmas and birthdays and going to the cinema."

"He'll ring up," said the friend. "You see. Next week. Tomorrow."

"Ah. Will he? Since when were birthdays always last week? And yellow trains."

"These trains . . ."

"Sorry about the trains." The girl saw sparrows float down from a tree and hop among crisp packets and paper bags. "He said it was a pity and we'd have to fix something another time. He ran out of coins and had to go."

Miles away, across roads and buses and taxis, the friend said, "Then that's how it is. Another time. There's always other times."

"I don't want other times," said the girl." I want yesterday. I want to be so happy like I was yesterday. I want to go back into yesterday and settle down there and live there for ever. I want to spend the rest of my life riding out of Clapham Junction on yellow trains, looking at the smoke against those clouds. I don't want to be here; I want to be there. I want to be sitting on those bright blue seats, watching the houses go by. I don't like now, I want to be then."

The friend sighed. "Go and eat that pizza. It won't keep."

'The ghost of a flea'

HE MET HER at the opening party for an exhibition of paintings by a friend of his brother's. He stood penned against a wall talking to no one with an empty glass in his hand and suddenly there was this short girl with a soft inexorable voice at his elbow, saying things.

"Sorry?"

"I said, you've got such a kind face, I knew you wouldn't mind my coming across. I mean, I can always tell, just looking at people. Most of them here – well, I just wouldn't . . . You see, the thing is . . ."

He couldn't hear the half of it. He bent over her, frowning with concentration. She had thick long fawn hair that sometimes obscured her face and a physical solidity at curious variance with some kind of manic tension. She alarmed him. She was called Angela. As the party thinned out he learned that they were going to have a curry at a place round the corner and then he would walk her back to her flat.

Over the curry, they exchanged telephone numbers. She said it was so lucky he was working in Holborn because actually her office was only just round the corner. She said she was terribly interested in painting, she'd done an art course once herself but as therapy in fact, it had been good, it had helped. After the meal, as they left, she said she was

77

feeling a bit odd. Hang on a minute, she said, do you mind? She stood on the pavement, her back against some railings, staring, it seemed, at the passing traffic, a small stocky girl with something dogged about her, dogged and enclosed. He wondered nervously if she was drunk, but she had had only a glass of lager with the curry. After a moment she said, "I'll be all right now, Paul, it's just I get this sort of breathlessness, it goes if I keep still a minute. Shall we go?" He left her outside the house in which she had a flat.

He was at home in the evening, five days later, when the phone rang. She said, "It's Angela. Look, can I come round? I'm having a bit of a bad spell, it's an awful help to talk."

He made her coffee. She took off her shoes and padded around his room with bare feet. She said, it must be marvellous to have so many books, I've got hardly any books. Is that Battersea? You must be able to see the river from this window, I never know if I love the river or if it upsets me.

She sat cross-legged on the rug with the coffee mug cradled in her hands, the thick dun swatches of her hair falling across her face, her soft quiet voice going on and on, unstoppable, distressing. "After Mummy and Daddy were killed in the car crash I lived with Daddy's aunt in Guildford until she got this liver disease. Then I got rheumatic fever and I was in St. Thomas's for nine months, because of the complications. They thought I was going to die and the thing is, it's left me with a sort of funny heart, but it's not too bad, they're terribly sweet, they see me every six months . . . Then I got the job with Hatchards and then I did the secretarial course and I went to Steers two years ago . . . I found this flat through my boss, he's been awfully kind . . . I'm taking Catholic instruction, I started with one of the fathers at Gregory Street but now I'm going to St. Damian's . . . I absolutely adore flying kites, I've got this new kite from Selfridges, I thought, let's go and fly it on Saturday, O.K.?"

He was disturbed, concerned. He said, "Haven't you got *any* relatives, Angela, honestly?"

She shook her head. "There's these people, the Stanleys, in Basingstoke, I go to at Christmas. Mrs Stanley was a friend of Mummy's. They've been terribly kind, I can go there any time, absolutely whenever I want."

They flew the kite on Hampstead Heath. It wriggled like a tethered serpent against the luminous London sky. Angela ran about, calling him. She wore a furry coat and boots, her face grew pink in the wind, she became quite pretty. Walking to the tube station, he wondered if she expected him to take her hand; he strode worriedly beside her, a tall stringy young man, short-sighted, good-tempered and made despondent by injustice. He did not find her sexually attractive. He told her at length of his work with a firm of architects in order to conceal and distance the guilt engendered by this absence of desire. He took her back to his rooms and made them scrambled eggs and bacon. Angela said, I can't cook, it's silly, I know, I've never learned, all the girls in my office are terribly good cooks. Later, she declared herself tired and lay on the sofa where she fell asleep. He sat in the darkening room, peering at newspapers, glancing at her from time to time in unease. He suspected she might be a rather unstable girl.

He met her for lunch in the pub near his office. They flew the kite again. Sometimes she telephoned him late in the evening and talked lengthily, fluently, her low regular voice coming to him through the noisy London night, tense and yet stoical. She made him think, uncomfortably and with a wrench of pity, of those resigned resilient children who stand at the edge of school playgrounds, unsought, excluded from games. She made him think also, disturbingly, of cripples. At that party, when first he met her, he had looked down, he now remembered, in instinctive search of something: a surgical boot, a leg caliper. You're being the most enormous help, Paul, she said. It's sweet of you to take so much trouble, you don't mind, do you? The thing is, I had this beastly business with someone at the office, I can't sleep, it's made me feel all strange, if I could just talk for a bit . . .

She said, I've never been to the Tate, isn't it silly? I had a thing about the river once, I used to keep going to the Embankment to walk up and down, and look over that bridge, the iron one – you know, which is it? – but I never went into the Tate. So I thought, let's go on Sunday. He said cautiously, Look Angela, there are these people I know with this cottage in Suffolk and I was actually thinking of going down there this weekend . . . She nodded and smiled her damaged smile and he winced and hurried on, but next week – next week would be fine.

She often arrived first at the pub or entrance to the Underground. She would have bought the drinks, the tickets, the sandwiches. No, she'd say, it's my turn, Paul, honestly, otherwise it's simply not fair and you've been so terribly sweet to me anyway, I'm not going to be any more of a nuisance.

He saw her from some way off, on the steps of the Tate, standing with her hands in her pockets and a strand of hair blown horizontally across her face, staring at the Thames. When he arrived she said, "Don't you think seagulls are the most terribly threatening things? Their eyes. When I was a child I used to have nightmares about birds."

In the Blake Room she pored over the cases. From time to time he lost her in the murky, crowded room and then would catch sight of her small bundled figure in a group, gazing at a picture, always looking somehow apart from other people, isolated. He joined her in front of a case of drawings at which she intently stared.

"Isn't that ridiculous!" she exclaimed. "*The Ghost of a Flea*! But that's mad – it's absurd. A flea couldn't have a ghost." She began to laugh, loudly. People turned their heads, peering across the dark, respectful room in which the paintings gleamed from their glass cases like tropical fish.

He tried to move her on. "Blake is a kind of visionary, isn't he? It's rather a neurotic picture. Isn't he supposed to have been a bit mad?"

"Neurotic!" She continued, mirthlessly, to laugh, "I hate it!"

"Let's go, then."

"Just a minute. Oh God, look at it – I'll never forget it, now. That awful grotesque head. It gives me the shivers."

"Come on, Angela," he said nervously.

"I'm coming. Can we go home?" She began to walk quickly towards the door.

He caught her up. "But it's only half past two. I thought we were going to . . ."

"I'm sorry, Paul, I'm not feeling too good." Her voice was even lower than usual. He loped behind her down the steps, out onto the Embankment. He thought she might be crying. The faint gloom always induced in him by her company was unsettlingly compounded now with both pity and irritation. At this time last week he had been having a convivial lunch in a Suffolk pub with an old friend and his jovial, matey wife. He said, "What's the matter, Angela?"

She was leaning now over the parapet, looking down at the viscous flow of the river. Seagulls bobbed among scarves of plastic. He peered at her. "You're not crying, are you?"

"I never cry. I can't remember ever crying. It was just that picture, it made me get this feeling I get."

"What sort of feeling?"

"I'm afraid it's almost impossible to explain to other people." She had her eyes closed, he now saw. "It's like being very scared, but you feel a bit as though you might faint as well. Your legs go funny. And you know it's only you who's like that, and there's nothing anybody else can do about it. I'll be fine in a minute. It's beginning to go now." She continued to hunch over the parapet.

Paul said, "You know, Angela, I wonder if perhaps it might be an idea to see a doctor sometime."

She opened her eyes and turned to look at him. She had brown, rather large eyes. "I have done."

"Ah. And . . . ?"

"What do you think?" she said wearily. "Look, Paul, I think I'm just about all right now, but I'd like to go back. Thank you for being so sweet. I'm sorry to be such a bore."

In silence they returned to her flat.

A week later she telephoned to ask him to come with her to a party.

"Tonight? Well, I'm not sure, Angela, truth to tell I've had a bit of a tiring day, would you mind awfully if . . ."

"Never mind. It's just it helps awfully having someone with me. And I wanted to talk to you anyway."

He sighed. "O.K. But only for a bit, if you don't mind."

At the party, she was in a state of uncharacteristic animation. She towed him around the room, locking in conversation with strangers, talking quickly and loudly, moving on. She drank rather a lot. Pink crests formed on her cheeks. When eventually they left she said, "Let's go back and have a cup of coffee at your place". He asked her what it was she had wanted to talk to him about and she said she couldn't remember, it didn't matter now.

In his room she sat as usual on the floor. She did a lot of yoga at one time, she had told him, and this inclination

82

was a legacy of that period. Similarly, a residual distaste for meat stemmed from having once been a vegetarian. She sat sipping coffee and telling him about Father Michael who was such a help and what he had said yesterday. Paul said, "When are you actually, er, going to be properly converted or whatever it's called?" She stared at him and replied, "Oh, I'm not, I've decided not to finish it, didn't I tell you? They've been terribly kind but I've decided to stop at the end of the month."

Presently she said, "I had too much to drink at that stupid party. I think I'd better spend the night here."

He shuffled in alarm. "But there's only my bed, Angela."

"I'll sleep on the sofa."

"I will, then. You have the bed."

"No. It's my own fault. I shouldn't have let those people keep filling my glass. I'm sorry, Paul. You go to bed. I'll just have a wash."

He retreated to the bedroom. Presently there was silence. With relief, he turned and slept.

He woke with a jump to see her standing in the doorway. "I can't sleep, I've got that awful feeling."

His heart sank. He sat up. "Look, Angela . . ."

She came over to the bed. "I'll get in with you. I'll just lie beside you and then I'll be fine. Go to sleep."

He said wildly, "Angela, I simply don't . . ."

"Go to sleep," she said again.

He rolled to the far side of the bed. She climbed in. He wasn't sure if she had any clothes on or not. He thought not. He thought she was stark naked six inches from him. He could feel warmth come across the sheet from her thigh. He cowered against the wall.

Presently he heard her breathe more heavily. She sighed, shifted, was asleep. He lay rigid, hour by hour. Once she sighed again and lurched towards him. He shrank into the crevasse between bed and wall where a cold draught strayed along his back.

In the morning, he wriggled precariously from the bed without touching her, grabbed his clothes and took them to the bathroom. When he was making tea and toast she came in wearing his dressing-gown. She said, "I feel such a fool. I feel such an awful stupid fool. I want to die."

He avoided her eye. "It's O.K., Angela, honestly, we were a bit overtired, that's all. Look, the marmalade's in the cupboard, shall I . . ."

"I wish I were dead."

He forced a laugh; it sounded even worse than he'd feared. "Oh come on, Angela, everyone has a bit too much every now and then, it's not . . ."

"Actually," she said, "I have tried to kill myself. Twice. I wasn't going to tell you."

He slopped the tea and did some concentrated diversionary wiping up.

"In fact," she said, "I probably would have told you. It's only fair, when you've been so sweet. The first time I took some pills and the second time I tried to jump into the river."

He dumped the cloth in the sink. "Tried?"

"There was this man who came along."

"Well," he said firmly, "I'm very glad it didn't work. And please don't talk like that, you'll feel fine later on, just you see. It's silly to get so upset. I'll have to rush now or I'll be late for the office. You'll be all right, won't you?"

She sat at the table, a small teddy-bearish figure in his brown schoolboy dressing-gown. She stared down at the table, her hair swathing her face. She did not answer.

"I'll give you a ring," he said desperately. "At lunch-time."

84

She looked at him. "That's very nice of you, Paul. I can't tell you what a help you are."

Outside, he took great gulps of the London morning. He paused at the shop further down the road outside which shocks of daffodils and tulips stood in buckets and he thought of buying her a bunch and going back and leaving them by the door, and then did not because flowers are no compensation for other unperformed actions, and in any case what he would be doing would be to assuage his own feelings, not make her any happier.

Either you take a shine to a girl or you don't. Unless of course you are the sort of bloke who is simply a sexual opportunist.

He shambled disconsolately to his office. He was twenty-seven. When he was nine he had written an indignant letter to the Prime Minister of the day protesting against stag-hunting, a barbarity which had just come to his attention and which had caused him a night of distress. Nowadays, he was the kind of person who gives up his seat to old ladies and contributes heavily to charities. He shambled to the office and at lunch-time he rang up Angela and the next evening he had a drink with her and at the weekend he went with her to a film.

Three weeks later, when the spring had just touched London, Paul fell in love. He met her in the house of some friends and at the end of another fifteen days they were in bed together. She was called Frances. She had dark curly hair and an exuberant personality. She was competent, generous, lithe and merry and she loved him back. He said, "Look, I'll have to tell you at some point, there's this girl. Not what you might think, not like that at all. The thing is, you see . . ." And then he cried, "Oh Christ, that's what she says – the thing is – it must be catching. But the thing is . . ."

85

He introduced Frances to Angela at the pub in which he had so often plied Angela with sandwiches (she always resisted food – it had struck him as curious that she remained so plump, there was in this also a hint about her of a determined survival against all the odds). Angela said, "I love your boots. I'd adore to wear ankle boots but my calves are too fat. Paul says you're a super cook. Can you teach me to make pizza? I've got this old schoolfriend coming to stay on Sunday and I want to make pizza for her. I thought, if you and Paul came on Saturday morning we could do it then and I could show you the street market round the corner. O.K.?"

They had planned to go to Greenwich that Saturday. As it was, Frances showed Angela how to make pizza till nearly three. Then Angela was feeling a bit low so they stayed till six or so to cheer her up. They never got to Greenwich. They went to a film in the evening and Frances said, "Angela's very nice, really, isn't she?" and Paul agreed that she was. Frances said, "It's the most awful shame," and Paul again agreed. They went to bed and had a lovely night and both, separately, thought once or twice of Angela and felt a trickle of guilt.

When Paul was not with Frances he conjured her from the pavement or the opposing row of faces in the Underground or from the pearly spring sky and dwelt upon her and told her what he was thinking and doing. He hovered over the telephone because to be about to speak to her was almost better than to be actually speaking to her and when she rang him he sometimes delayed answering because the sound of her voice induced such pleasure that it was really almost impossible to do anything but savour it.

Sometimes the voice was not Frances's but Angela's and then he would be hearty and welcoming and if necessary – and it frequently was – concerned. He advised and sympathised and reassured. Angela said, "I think it's marvellous about Frances and you, I do like her so much," and he muttered that Frances liked her too, naturally, of course. Angela said, "What do you think she wants for her birthday?" and Paul said he didn't know, he'd try to find out. In the end he went with Angela to choose a very expensive iron casserole which he knew she could not afford. Frances also knew this, and thereafter the casserole glimmered at them from Frances's kitchen shelf, inducing discomfort.

Once, they were in Frances's bed when the telephone rang. It was half past midnight. Frances said, "Oh lor, I hope that's not poor Auntie Liz died, Mum said she'd ring." She was gone five minutes. When she returned she said, "It's Angela. She tried you first and then supposed you were here. She sounds in the most awful state, poor thing. Something about a picture. Do talk to her, Paul."

He stood shifting from one bare foot to the other on a stone floor and Angela told him she was seeing these heads, these monstrous heads and she thought she would go mad. She said her doorbell had rung and she'd gone to answer it and there'd been no one there but she'd seen this silhouette of someone going down the stairs with a head like – like that ghastly picture. The teeth, she said, those teeth. That eye. Picture? he queried, flexing his toes, drawing Frances's cotton dressing-gown round his thighs, what picture? Oh, *The Ghost of a Flea*. But honestly, Angela, that's ridiculous, I mean you must *know*, really and truly, it was a trick of the light. You're having nightmares. And from far away across streets and buildings Angela's quiet and level voice told him of voids and chasms and a world that was only partly comprehensible and when presently she paused and for moments he could not hear her he said sharply "Angela? Are you still there?"

When he came back to bed Frances said, "Do you think she'll be all right? I sort of felt we ought to have gone over there; or one of us anyway." And for a while they lay in unease until they slept and in the morning they phoned her, early. She said she was a little better now but tired. At the weekend she came to see them, bearing a strange primeval plant which subsequently died in a protracted manner. She said she was sorry she'd been so silly but she sometimes got like that and there was absolutely nothing you could do about it. The time when she'd taken all those pills had been when she'd got like that. She said it made all the difference having them there, knowing that all she had to do was pick up the phone. She said they'd been so sweet.

Paul and Frances had planned to go to Brighton for the day and in the end Angela came with them. They walked between the green sea and the sparkling stucco and Angela talked about the school she'd been at and the friend she'd had there that she'd lost touch with now and the new woman in the office who didn't like her, she knew. She walked with her eyes on the pavement through the air that brushed the face like clouds of feathers, under a sky pegged to the horizon by tiny cut-out ships, past murmurous glistening shingle and piers sending long dainty fingers of white ironwork into the milky surf. She passed through all this inside the dark capsule of her own head. Frances said, honestly Angela I should forget about that, I mean it's years ago and as for the woman in the office she sounds an old cow, just don't take any notice of her. And Angela smiled her separate smile, her smile from an unshared world and said, yes, Frances, you're absolutely right, of course, you're so sensible, yes, that's what I must do.

Look at Royal Crescent, said Paul, it's very famous, architecturally, isn't it handsome?

Just a little bit like lavatory tiles, suggests irreverent

Frances, skipping aside from the lecture that this provokes. And Angela looks with her shuttered eyes and says yes, isn't it pretty, when did you say it was built Paul?

They ate a fish tea and rode back to London in a train that stitched its way through the Sussex fields. Gorgeous, said Frances, heavenly, let's live in that house – no, that one. And Angela talked of this man she know who lived in Burgess Hill, who played the flute, and said she felt better now, quite a bit, she'd sleep tonight, she thought, she'd take a pill and have a good night.

Spring opened into summer. Paul and Frances went again to Brighton, alone, and Frances's skin turned a pale coffee colour and Paul wondered if the day would ever come when he could be with her and stop looking at her. He knew now that he would marry her, if this plan fitted in with her intentions, which he rather thought it would, and he woke every morning in a state of astonishment. He could not imagine why he should have been selected for such incredible happiness, there must be some mistake, he had no right.

They were in Paul's room, late one evening, when the phone went. Frances, sleepily, fondly, watched him press the receiver to his ear, scowling, listened to him saying, "Yes, Hello? Hello? *Hello*".

Put it down, she said, it's a wrong number. And then he was frowning more. "Angela? I can hardly hear, can you talk loudly. What? Angela, where are you?" There was a pause. Frances sighed and sat up. Paul said urgently, "Stay there. What's the number – I'll ring you back." He looked over at Frances. "She's in a phone box somewhere, she sounds awful, she says there's some man following her. She's talking about killing herself."

Frances said, "Oh God." They stared at each other for a moment. Paul dialled.

Faintly, insistently, Angela's voice whispered into the room. Paul said, "Yes. Yes. Yes, I see." And then, "No, no, Angela, don't – stay where you are."

Frances stood up. She fetched pencil and paper, handed them to Paul. She watched Paul talk, scribble, talk. As he put the receiver down she was putting on her coat.

They saw the phone box from some way off, a brown figure huddled within it. Behind, the river glittered away to left and right, a carnival of lights and rosy floodlit buildings. When Angela saw them she came out of the phone box and stood in front of them with her hands in her pockets. She said, "The man came again, the man in that drawing. He followed me and every time I turned round I saw his face, that awful face. I went up onto the bridge and he was still there. I was going to jump in."

They steered her to a taxi. They took her back to Frances's flat. She went to bed in Frances's bed. Paul went home.

The next day Frances said to him, "I think this is going to drive me bananas. Quite honestly." After a moment she went on, "Do you think she ever would?"

"Kill herself?"

She nodded.

"I don't know," said Paul. "You read things in newspapers. About – you know – cries for help and that sort of stuff."

"Some of them actually do."

They stared at each other.

Paul said, "I'm sorry, darling. It's me who landed her on you. On us. But you can't just . . ."

"No. I know you can't. That's the whole point."

Paul and Frances went to Cornwall for a holiday. They walked for miles on shaggy cliff paths and waded into icy seas and made incessant love and arranged to marry in the autumn. They sent Angela a postcard of lobster pots and a shiny unreal sea. On the day they returned to London they found a note from her at Frances's flat with a basket of fruit and a bottle of wine. A few days later they met her for a drink and she was animated, sprightly, and talked of this girl she'd met who she might go to Portugal with later on. They told her about the wedding and she said I think that's marvellous, how super, you will invite me *won't* you? She asked Frances to come shopping with her and help her buy some clothes. Afterwards, Frances said she seems fine, doesn't she? I mean really much better, more together, more . . .

"More like other people?"

"That, I suppose."

"The terrible thing," said Paul after a moment, "about Angela, the terribly sad thing, is that she is only just one notch away from being, well, perfectly all right. To lots of people most of the time she probably does seem fine."

"Quite."

They were silent, with separate and similar visions of Angela's small resolute figure, forging on, alone, possessed, unreachable.

The London summer ripened and the streets flowed with tourists and Paul redecorated Frances's flat as a preliminary to married life therein. He moved, gradually, his few possessions and spent long hours in the meticulous application of paint to walls and ceilings with the windows open to the warm clattering evenings. He had never been prone to religious belief except once briefly in adolescence when he had been smitten by the personality of the new school chaplain. Now, in the tranquillity of his happiness, he looked for someone to whom to offer thanks; it seemed irrational that all this should have come to him from a void. Frances cooked him exquisite meals with the minimum of fuss.

It was in the midst of one such evening that a call came from St. Thomas's Hospital. Were they, a voice wanted to know, Miss Frances Bennett and Mr Paul Freeland?

In apprehension and with gathering expectation Frances replied that they were. She knew now what would come next, and Paul, the paintbrush arrested in mid-stroke, looked across the room, met her eyes and experienced for the first time that wordless communication of married people: he read her. When she put the phone down he said, "Angela." Frances nodded.

At the entrance to the hospital ward a sister briskly held them. "Miss Bennett and Mr Freeland? For Angela Holywell? She's in the end bed. She gave you as next of kin. I gather there are no parents or anything. You'll find her fairly comfortable now, a bit dopy still. She was asking just now if you were coming, she specially wants to see you. I shouldn't stay too long."

"What exactly," said Paul, "happened? They just said . . ."

"Sleeping pills. The usual. Not enough, fortunately, and she'd left the door of her flat ajar for some reason and a neighbour came in with a message."

They sat on either side of the high hospital bed in which Angela lay propped up on pillows. Her hair had been brushed and lay in two neat hanks down each side of her face. She wore a flannelette nightgown sprigged with small blue flowers. She looked rather younger than twenty-seven. She held their hands in her own small, surprisingly powerful grip and said, "Don't let go for a minute – d'you mind? Just for a minute. It was sweet of you to come. The thing is – I'd been seeing that man again, you know, the picture – for days and days now. I couldn't stand it any longer. You must think I'm an awful fool."

Paul said, "The man doesn't exist, Angela. It's just a picture."

"I know. Oh, I know. There's always been something, you see. Voices, sometimes. There always will be. But I think I'll be all right now – they've been terribly nice to me here. There's this doctor – he's coming in to see me again tomorrow. And it makes all the difference just knowing you're there, both of you. You didn't mind me giving them your names, do you? You're not annoyed?"

And Paul and Frances said that no, of course they weren't annoyed and of course they didn't mind. The grip of Angela's small warm hands slackened but her low voice continued to narrate and explain and Paul and Frances looked at each other across the bed, both separated and tethered by her, perplexed and saddened and sharing a spectral, queasy vision of what was yet to come.

The art of biography

SHE WAS EIGHTY if she was a day. Which of course was to be expected: Edward Lamprey would be eighty-seven if he were still alive and the daughter had said Miss Rockingham was a contemporary. Miss Lucinda Rockingham. A curiously lavish name for the spare, slightly bent old lady who stood now in her doorway, looking up at him.

He put out a hand, smiled his charming open young man's smile. "Miss Rockingham? I'm Malcolm Sanders. It's so good of you to let me take up your time like this."

Twenty-eight interviews, duly recorded and filed. Seventeen card index boxes. Seven hundred and nineteen letters in the British Library and the University of Texas and in God knows how many box files and drawers of desks. Notes and footnotes and references and cross-references; checks and cross-checks and headings and sub-headings. Names and places and times and dates. All sewn up and stashed away, or just about. A man's life reduced to paper and print – or rather, card and tempo pen. The material, the valuable laboriously gathered material for the definitive biography of Edward Lamprey, poet and man of letters, born eighteen-ninety-three, died nineteen-fifty-eight.

He yawned, discreetly, into the back of his hand, turning momentarily aside as though to admire the view of the estuary beyond the wide window of Lucinda Rockingham's sitting-room. A flat, melancholy East Anglian view, all sea and sky and fleeing birds and, far away, cars twinkling along the coast road. Bleak and impersonal, as was the house bleak and impersonal – an Edwardian villa, faintly hostile from without and chilly within, the sofa too hard, the room too neat, the pictures too square upon the walls.

And Lucinda Rockingham an agreeable enough old thing but not of any use, he could tell within the first five minutes, nothing of any significance to say about Lamprey ("He was a great poet, you know, Mr Sanders, yes, I knew him since nineteen-forty, yes, he visited this house . . ."), the trip a waste.

He smiled and jotted the odd note and let his mind drift. He examined his feelings – took them out and prodded them, held them up to the light, took their temperature, and they were the same. He was in love, no two ways about it. Conjure her up, right here on the worn patterned carpet beside the unlit Rayburn Maxistove, and there was that delicious liquefaction of the vitals. He smiled and made another note and held her in his arms, against his cheek, her mouth . . . Better phone as soon as he was through here, before she left the office, there was a phone booth on the sea-front, he'd just catch her if he cut this short . . .

That, actually, was the funny thing about Lamprey. The one odd, unsatisfactory blank. Love. For a man whose passionate nature spun from every line of the poems, the absence of any evidence that he ever experienced intensity of love was curious to say the least of it. Certainly there'd been none in the marriage, probably not even at the very beginning. A haphazard union that drifted into a convenient arrangement for the upbringing of the four cherished daughters. For them, certainly, there had been love, devotion indeed, but not the kind of love to account for the depth of feeling that lurked in the poetry, the pastoral poems in particular that read at times like something quite other, like . . .

". . . occasionally helped with some of the more tedious clerical tasks," said the old lady. "The study of Coleridge, which I daresay you know . . ." She smoothed the cotton print dress across her knees and smiled, a rather sweet smile, a beauty once probably – no, not a beauty, just a very pretty woman (no husband, apparently, odd, that) – and bless her yes one did indeed know the study of Coleridge, every chapter and verse of it, what did she imagine one had spent three years doing for heavens' sake? The daughters had had some vague idea that she did odd bits of secretarial stuff for Lamprey, that sort of thing – the kind of useful friend a man like that sometimes attracts. But they'd not known much about her, none of them, only as a name that cropped up once or twice, hadn't suggested her until this late point, with everything ready to be written, the first three chapters drafted indeed. And then she had to be looked into, of course, just in case. Another index card, another reference.

He got up. He beamed. He thanked. He took her warm, dry small hand and thanked again. He went out to the car got in, looked back, waved, started the engine, glanced down at the AA road book open on the seat beside him.

And there she was suddenly at the car window, a little breathless, saying something he could not quite catch.

He switched the engine off.

"Letters?"

"Letters, Miss Rockingham?"

She hadn't known whether to mention, had wondered if it were perhaps better . . . had thought suddenly, seeing him about to go, had decided that no, really, that it would be wrong, that . . .

About two hundred letters, she thought. Upstairs. In two shoeboxes. No, three shoeboxes.

"Letters to whom, Miss Rockingham?"

To her. All of them. Two hundred.

They went back into the house. Upstairs. Into a spare bedroom with a whiff of damp to it and the sense of being for many years unslept in. And out of a cupboard came the boxes.

"If you would like to have a glance," she said, "to see if you might wish to make use of them. They are in chronological order."

He took the first letter from the envelope. ". . . Until I saw you come into the room yesterday," wrote Lamprey, "I never understood the meaning of delight. I have never, until now, delighted. I have seen, since then, again and again, the door open and you walk in and my whole being has surged upwards. I cannot endure to wait until . . ."

He put the letter down and looked at her.

"Edward Lamprey and I," she said, a little stiffly, "loved each other for many years."

"Christ," said the girl. "How weird. I mean, how absolutely extraordinary. I bet you're thrilled."

"Hang on – I'll put another ten pence in. Hello? The thing is she won't let them out of the house which is fair enough but she's willing for me to make copies and thank God she's got an old typewriter so I can get going right away. She's extraordinarily helpful – set up a table for me and fussed round with electric fires and whatnot and now she's cooking us some sumptuous meal. Routed out some pajamas, even."

"Oh," she said. "I see. So you won't . . ."

"No. Not this weekend. And I wanted to see you. I've been thinking about it all day. Hello?"

"Yes. I'm still here. Oh, well . . ."

"Thursday was – just incredible."

"What?"

"I said Thursday was marvellous."

"Yes," she said. "Wasn't it. I've been thinking too . . . Oh, bother. Never mind. How long do you think it'll take?"

"I don't know. they're long letters. Actually, they're beautiful. The most beautiful letters I've ever read. Love letters. They're – oh God I can't explain. It's going to change the book entirely, finding this. It's changed Lamprey. I feel – oh, really involved for the first time. It's not just work any more, I actually care about him as a person. Oh, Christ, that's the last ten pence – look, I'll ring again tomorrow. O.K.?"

She stood in the doorway with a towel over one arm, and a pair of blue and white striped pajamas. "I got these out for you, Malcolm. I think they would be about the right size."

Lamprey's?

"My brother," said Lucinda, "stayed here for several months before his death. Some of his things have not yet been cleared out." She looked in sudden doubt at the pajamas. "But perhaps you would rather not. They have of course been laundered."

He held out his hand. "It's very kind of you. In fact the whole thing is extraordinarily kind. I can't tell you how grateful I am."

"It would be as well," she said, "to go to the chemist for the shaving things before they close. I thought we might take some sherry together at about seven, before we eat. There are one or two points I have thought of that may interest you."

There was sherry, good sherry at that, and whisky and gin and a soda siphon, magicked from heaven knows where in this surprising house. And Lucinda Rockingham wearing now some long velvet dressing-gown-like garment, looking pink and frail and yet, when it came to conversation, animated. And the Rayburn Maxistove had been lit and there was this extraordinarily good smell coming from the kitchen.

It was midnight before he went to bed. She had left him at eleven or so and he had sat on looking through the bundle of letters he would copy out the next day and, finally, reading some of Lamprey's poems. *The Cycle of the Year* sequence, written shortly after he met Lucinda Rockingham and which, knowing what one now knew, took on a new meaning. Overhead, boards delicately creaked, and presently there was silence. Outside, the occasional car rustled through the rain. He put the letters away, went to bed, lay awake for a while consumed with erotic yearnings, and fell asleep to dream of Lucinda Rockingham bicycling once, as she had described, along the waterfront with Edward Lamprey. A dog had run in front of his bike, causing him to fall and sprain an ankle. He had walked back to the house supported by Lucinda's arm. They had known one another, at that point, Lucinda thought, six weeks or so. Malcolm felt, in his dream, the touch of Lucinda's hand upon Lamprey's arm; he walked, with Lamprey, in a blaze of love.

"The amazing thing is," he said, "that they only saw each other at most every few months. Usually they met in London and every now and then he came down here. Her mother was alive then, and living with her so they weren't even alone that much if he came to the house. And then all the letters . . . Honestly, I wish I could . . . I'd love to read some of them to you. They're some of the best stuff he ever wrote."

"You certainly seem very involved in it all."

There was a pause.

"What are you doing?" he said. "At this minute. Apart from talking to me. So I can imagine."

"I'm looking out of the window. There's a white cat walking along the window ledge opposite. It's pouring with rain."

"It's chucking down here too. What are you wearing?"

"Oh, goodness," the girl said. "A sort of blue shirt thing. And jeans. How's it going – I mean apart from being good and all that – how much longer will it take?"

"Another week at least. I can't see any way of getting through before."

"Oh, gosh," she said.

He read and typed and the old lady brought him coffee and occasionally aspirin. Twice, they walked down to the sea, he with his hand hovering beside her arm across the roads. Edward Lamprey, she said, had loved to walk along the beach collecting driftwood. Yes, she said, the poem 'Sea-shapes' was written after such a walk and yes, she supposed the references were more particular than might be supposed. She talked of a concert at the Maltings to which they had been together and of meetings in London, always with some shared activity in mind, visits to art galleries and places of interest and walks in Kew Gardens and Richmond Park. Lucinda Rockingham stayed with a cousin in Putney; Lamprey had a room in a friend's flat in Fulham which he used when in London. Each September they went to a Prom; in the spring they took the steamer to Greenwich.

And the letters, one upon another, a passionate narrative of love and commitment.

No, she said, we never travelled together. It would not have been possible. I had my mother to think of for

many years; Edward took his family always to Cornwall.
No, I never met his daughters; he talked of them a great
deal, they were very close, I have a photograph of them
when Marion was twelve and the others of course a little
younger.

Year after year; through autumns and winters and springs
and summers; moving from one longed-for, hoarded time
to another.

She spoke of Lamprey's eclectic tastes, in music and in
literature. She took down from the bookshelves the copies
annotated in his hand, passages scored in the familiar red
ink ("He used the same fountain pen for twelve years."),
observations scribbled in the margins ("I have to confess
that I never liked Edward's habit of defacing books, albeit
with the best of intentions"). She peered into the intestines
of the shining mahogany box in the corner, fiddled with
slow crooked fingers, tutted and exclaimed, and produced,
astonishingly, Duke Ellington and Sydney Bechet.

The rain turned to sunshine and the sunshine fell in wide
mossy shafts upon the growing pile of letters on the deal
table in the spare bedroom. Upon gaiety and sadness and
delight and regret. Upon eighteen years.

"Soft lights and sweet music!" said the girl. "New Orleans
and Eartha Kitt! Well, I never! What's a radiogram, by the
way? I must say, if she wasn't eighty I'd feel I'd been cut
out."

"My head's spinning. I've been at it six hours on the trot.
I got so absorbed I didn't even hear her bring me in tea. It
got cold. The cucumber sandwiches went soggy."

"All this vicarious experience. I don't know . . ."

"I had this dream about you last night."

"What was I doing?"

"I couldn't possibly tell you. It was disgraceful."

"Now, now," she said. Winds sighed and whistled across four counties.

"What?"

"I didn't say anything."

"It's ten days," he said, "since Thursday. Ten days and – six and a half hours."

"Look," said the girl, "I *know*. Don't I know."

"When I see you, I'm just going to . . ."

"I can't hear."

"It doesn't matter. At least it does. Darling."

"Listen," she said. "Have a break for a day or two. Come to London. You could always go straight back."

"No," he said. "No, I can't. I want to – goodness, I want to – but I can't. I'm right in the middle of it. You see there's something I just can't . . . There's an enormous thing I simply don't . . . Hello? Are you there?"

Miss Rockingham, in the interests of literary history I have to ask you if your relationship with the poet was a physical one?

Miss Rockingham, did you sleep with the man or did you not?

Perhaps, he told himself, it doesn't matter. So far as the book is concerned, it need never be stated. Prurience, after all, is only an arm's length away. The letters matter; the relationship matters; let the rest be silence.

But I need to know. For myself, not for the book. Because. Because I have read the letters and humbly experienced through them the feelings of Edward Lamprey and seen with the eyes of Edward Lamprey the woman he loved. Because I care.

They sat up late, with the radiogram turned low, and Lucinda Rockingham opened a bottle of madeira, a relic of her brother. She poured the madeira into crystal glasses

off which the lamplight snapped, and talked of the onset
of Lamprey's illness, of an afternoon in London when she
had, for the first time, understood that he was dying. An
exhibition at the Tate, she said. She turned the glass in her
fingers and light flew from it into the corners of the room.
Chagall, I remember, and Kandinsky.

"It seems a bit creepy to me," said the girl.

"You see I honestly do not know. I think it's quite possible
they didn't. Which makes it all the more remarkable. The
letters. All of it."

"I don't mean them. I mean you."

"Sorry?"

"You seem," she said resentfully, "to find them more
compelling than real life."

He delved frantically in his pocket; the coin clunked.
"Hello? It's O.K., I've put another one in . . . You sound
cross. Please don't sound cross."

"I'm not," she said, "cross."

"Actually, I love you. What? I said, I *love* you."

"Oh . . .," she said at last, "Oh, Malcolm."

"And I keep thinking . . ."

"Yes?"

"Oh, just . . . I keep thinking about us."

"You keep thinking," the girl said, "that we haven't been
to bed together either?"

The pile of letters diminished. Lucinda Rockingham, standing at his elbow with a proffered cup of coffee said, "Dear
me, I shall soon be losing you. One more day? Two more
days?"

"Three, I think. Saturday should finish it. I'm never
going to be able to thank you enough for all this."

"It has been a pleasure," she said graciously. "I've

enjoyed your company. I lead a solitary life these days. I has done me good to talk. I hope I have not talked too much."

"Oh, goodness . . . I don't know quite honestly when I've been more fascinated. You've – well, you've just changed everything for me, so far as the book is concerned. I only hope you will be happy with it, eventually. That you won't, um . . ."

"Have any regrets?" said Miss Rockingham. "I think not. I've thought it all over and am certain I made the right decision. It is what Edward would have wished. Now that his wife is no longer alive. So – Saturday will be our last evening together."

"Thank goodness you rang. I was so terrified you might not. Listen, the most incredible thing. You know that friend of mine – the girl who plays in an orchestra at Snape? Well, she's driving down on Saturday and she said why not come along? Several of them have got this cottage and there's a room I could have for the night."

"That's amazing," he said. "That's wonderful."

"So what do you think? Shall I . . ."

"Is this room a big room?"

"Actually," she said, "I think it is quite a big room."

There were seventeen letters left. He read them through, in order, one after another, until the last. The final three were written from the nursing home in which Lamprey died.

There was no indication. Nothing to confirm, one way or another. Just as throughout.

"A cup of tea," said Lucinda Rockingham. "Earl Grey this morning. Edward had leanings towards Earl Grey. A small point I had forgotten to mention."

He pulled the typewriter towards him, smoothing out the one-hundred-and-seventy-sixth letter.

"We should hit Aldeburgh," the girl said, "at about six. So where shall we meet?"

"I'll ring you at this cottage place. Does it have a number?"

"Yes. Hang on. Here it is . . ."

"O.K. I've got that. Sixish? Wonderful. Twenty-four hours."

"I know. I can't believe it."

"I can't either. Yes, I can. I'm about ten years older, incidentally. Since the week before last."

"Silly . . .," she said. "How's it going, by the way?"

"Practically gone. All tied up, nearly."

"Have you found out if . . ."

"No." He looked through the glass of the phone box at grey sea marshalled beyond the sedate lamp-posts of the esplanade, at the back of a cast-iron bench, at the cold eye of a sea-gull. "No, I haven't."

"Does it still matter?"

"Yes," he said. "It does."

"Couldn't you ever so discreetly ask?"

"Christ, no."

"I have been thinking," said Lucinda Rockingham, "that in view of the fact that this is your last evening we might have a little celebration. I have ordered a duck from the butcher and I find that happily there is a bottle of what seems to be quite a nice wine in the storeroom."

"Oh . . . Oh, that's terribly kind but in fact as it happens a friend of mine . . ."

"You were intending to stay overnight?"

"Well, I had been going to suggest actually that . . ."

"It has occurred to me that now you have read all

106

the letters there may be one question that is bothering you."

He stared at her – neat, old, bent, her eyes bright amid a soft tissue of wrinkles. "Well – yes. Yes, there is – there is something I had been wondering about."

"This evening," said Miss Rockingham. "This evening over our little celebration, I think might be a suitable time."

"Oh," he said. "You've come. You're here. Did you have a good drive down?"

"I think so. I hardly noticed. Where are you?"

"In the phone box on the sea-front."

"Then you can drive over in about ten minutes. Look, I'll tell you how to get here, it's a turning off the coast road just after . . ."

A sea-gull gawped at him again, from the wall, with a metallic eye. "I tried to ring you in London. You'd gone. You see, the thing is she says . . ." The sea-gull raised its bill to the white sky and shouted; he could hardly hear his own words, his inexplicable inexcusable words ". . . so you see I must, I simply must. Shall I ring you say at eleven or so? She goes to bed then."

"I'm not sure," the girl said eventually, "that I'll be here. I may go over to Snape with Diana."

"Well, I'll try, shall I, all the same?"

"You can try," she said.

Miss Rockingham feared the duck was perhaps a little tough but thought the wine adequate. She allowed him to clear the table and moved with her still half-full glass into the sitting-room. She opened the front of the Rayburn Maxistove and stabbed energetically at the coals within. She sat down.

"You have presumably wondered about the nature of my

relationship with Edward Lamprey. We were never lovers. In the physical sense."

"Oh," he said. "Yes. Quite. I see. Not that I . . . There would really be no reason to . . . For the purposes of the book."

"It was agreed between us. On account of his family. And now that that point is out of the way shall we have some music?"

Later, much later, when she was in bed, he walked down to the phone box. Youths with motorbikes revelled on the esplanade, spilling from the pubs; a small white dog trotted purposefully past the darkened shop fronts; the sea slapped against a jetty. He dialled the girl's number. When it had rung a dozen times he put the receiver down and examined his feelings. He felt nothing, nothing at all. Just a faint regret, a pale decreasing sense of loss.

What the eye doesn't see

THE MISSES KNIGHT, Joyce and Nora, on the threshold of old age, lived in a large Georgian house in Pershore, Worcestershire. Pershore is one of those medium-sized market towns that give an impression of slight detachment from the present, despite such normalities as supermarkets, petrol stations and billboards. Something to do with the symmetry of eighteenth century brick façades, perhaps, and side streets secluded from the thunder of through traffic. The Knights' house, number seven St. Joseph's Place, was in just such a side street, or cul-de-sac, rather, and here the detachment achieved was quite remarkable.

There was little to tether the house to year or even decade: no recent electrical appliance or quickly identifiable piece of decor, no contemporary books, no magazines or periodicals. The Misses Knight had achieved a selective repudiation of the society in which they lived; they took what they wanted, such as Bendicks chocolates, Bath Oliver biscuits, main drainage, antibiotics and insecticides, the protection of the law and a constant supply of heat, light and water, and rejected the rest. What the eye doesn't see, the heart doesn't grieve over, they said; Nora and Joyce had trained the eye to see only what it wished to see, and the heart to restrict its concern. We know very little, they would say, about what is going on; we lead our own lives.

They took *The Times*, of course, for the Hatches, Matches and Despatches, as Nora called them. She would run her eye carefully down the columns every day at breakfast, in search of a relevant name. "Someone called Lucy Symington got married. Do you think that could be anything to do with Molly Symington?" They pondered. "A daughter couldn't be as young as that," said Nora. "Grand-daughter if anything." Molly Symington had been at school with them. The address gave no clue; in any case they had not communicated for forty years. "A John Chalmers died. Eighty-nine. Weren't those people on holiday at Salcombe called Chalmers? The father, perhaps." Nobody had been born who could be linked in any way to their own lives. Joyce folded the paper up carefully, for consignment to the fire-lighting pile in the pantry.

The house was called Cader Idris, in fond tribute to that part of Wales in which the sisters had spent the war years, in retreat from such dangers and aggravations as seemed bound to interfere with normal life in Hove, where they were living in 1939. It was a wise decision; in Dolgelly it had been possible – except for nuisances like rationing, black-out and lack of petrol – more or less to ignore what was going on elsewhere. They had had a good war; Nora taught herself petit point and Joyce grew irises with notable success. A photograph of the iris border in May 1943, a blaze of *I. xiphium* and *I. laevigata*, had been printed in *Country Life* – a heady moment. It hung now, framed, over the bureau in the drawing-room. They had done a little war-work with the local WVS, because one really should show willing. And had acquired a taste for King Charles spaniels, the latest in a long line of which lay now in a patch of sunlight on the Turkish rug, flopping his tail around in expectation.

"Let Ben have a bikky," said Nora. "And then put him outside."

French windows opened from the breakfast-room onto the terrace and large walled garden. The garden was re-markable. Although right in the centre of Pershore it was half an acre or so in size; an aerial view would have shown it, like the grounds of Buckingham Palace, as a startling green oasis amid roofs and roads, an unsuspected haven. The walls were so high and thick that although on one side traffic passed within a few yards of the herbaceous border, the lilac walk and the rose garden, one was barely con-scious of its presence; the occasional rattle or bump, blast of a horn, jangle of an ambulance, served only to emphasize the island seclusion of number seven. And yet only a few minutes away were the conveniences of the High Street: Boots, W.H. Smith, Sainsbury's. Not, of course, that Joyce and Nora did the household shopping themselves – that was done by the housekeeper. They employed a housekeeper and lady gardener, both resident in the west portion of the house beyond the kitchens, which was converted into a self-contained unit. Mr Knight had been a textile manufacturer; the firm had boomed in the fifties with the development of artificial fibres. His daughters' capital, cushioned and bolstered almost literally by dralon, courtelle, terylene, polyester and so forth, had kept up nicely with inflation. They were still quite com-fortable, thank goodness. Which makes all the difference, as Joyce said, between being able to lead one's own life as one wants and having to get involved with things one wouldn't care for.

The housekeeper and lady gardener were a couple called Beryl and Sylvia. They had turned out to be an excellent arrangement, being close friends so that, as Joyce was fond of telling people, there was none of that friction so common

111

between two women working together. It was a harmonious household.

Joyce and Nora made certain sorties to the High Street themselves: to the library, Debenhams, and The Cake Shop. They both had a sweet tooth. Tea was the pinnacle of the day. The lingering decisions between cream-topped cherry tarts, macaroons, chocolate fancies, eclairs, meringues and slices of coffee gateau enriched each afternoon. They took it in turns to go out for the cakes. Otherwise they remained for much of the time in St. Joseph's Place. Occasionally they attended local functions, but did not take an active part in the life of the town. The complaints of their acquaintances and contemporaries about change and desecration left them unmoved; they did not themselves much notice such things. When they found their route to the park made disagreeable by the building of a housing estate, they simply took Ben round a different way, avoiding the mud and rubble. The new multi-storey car park had been in the process of erection nine months before it caught their eye from the spare room window, blocking the view of the Abbey, which was a pity. Joyce ran up some net curtains, a pretty flounced nylon from Debenhams.

Beryl and Sylvia were efficient, cheerful, and kept themselves to themselves. They did their work and sat over the television of an evening; its muted quacking could be heard from behind their sitting-room door. Nora and Joyce also had a television set, on which they watched nature programmes, serializations of classic novels, 'Gardeners' World' and the weather forecast. Joyce had made a small art of switching on at precisely the right moment to catch the forecaster's opening words without being subjected to the closing paragraphs of the news. Beryl and Sylvia, on the other hand, watched things like Panorama and Man Alive, and sometimes, tiresomely, tried to initiate conversations about politicians and strikes and some bother in the Middle East. Joyce had to be a bit firm about that sort of intrusion, but on the whole they were nice types, and Beryl was an excellent cook. Beryl was the dominant partner, a small dark woman, her wiry black hair suggesting Welsh blood. She sang in the Abbey choir. They had been at St. Joseph's Place for three years now.

In view of which, and the generally good relationship, the Misses Knight had felt inclined to go along with Beryl's request, made as she cleared the breakfast things one morning. Even so, they exchanged wary glances.

"How old?" asked Joyce.

The niece was eleven, apparently. Joyce and Nora nodded with relief: a younger child, of course, would have been out of the question. A quiet little thing, Beryl asserted. You'll hardly know she's there, through in our part, she won't touch anything in the garden, Sylvia'll see to that. And it'll give my sister and her husband the chance of a break on their own, ten days in the Italian Lakes, I mean, it's no fun for a child, that sort of trip, they took Tracy to Spain last year and she was bored stiff, and tummy upsets and all that. So I said Sylvia and I'd have her, this once. Well, thank you very much then, Miss Knight, as I say she'll be no bother at all, we'll see she stays put our side of the house.

And indeed when the time came Nora and Joyce were not even aware of the child's arrival for the first three days of her presence at Cader Idris. She came to Joyce's attention, eventually, as a shadowy extension of Beryl on the stairs, gathering up the trailing end of some dirty sheets that her aunt was carrying, so that Beryl, for a moment, looked like a bride with ghostly attendant. Joyce jumped and exclaimed. Beryl said, "Say how do you do to Miss Knight, Tracy. She's been giving me a hand with the laundry. Right, I'll have those pillowcases now."

She was a very thin child. Knobs stuck out all over her, ac-
centuated by the clinging material of her jersey and trousers:
hip-bones, the swoop of collar-bones, spiky shoulders, fur-
rowing of ribs, small discs of nipples. A bit pasty, too. The
kind of child, Joyce thought, that needed fresh country air
and cod liver oil. Memories stirred, of evacuees in Wales
during the war. But this was no East End waif: Tracy's father,
one had been told, was quite high up in a frozen food firm.
They had a four bedroomed house and two cars. Joyce said
kindly, "Hello, Tracy. I hope you're enjoying your holiday."

The girl was watching her with small, sharp, observant
eyes, the narrowed look of a reflective cat, a little disconcerting. She tugged her aunt's arm and whispered something.
Beryl laughed. "Tracy was wondering if she could come
and see the china dogs in the drawing-room. She noticed
them from the terrace through the window and thought
they were really pretty."

In front of the china cabinet Joyce said instructively,
"They are a kind of china called Staffordshire. They used to
belong to my mother."

"Are they valuable?"

"Yes, I suppose so."

"My mum's got a glass vase she got in Venice that cost
fifteen pounds." Tracy was standing on one leg now,
scratching the back of her knee with the other, an irritating
contortion. "Excuse my saying so, Miss Knight, but you've
got a smudge on your cheek." She watched with detached
interest as Joyce, ruffled, scrubbed at her face with a hand-
kerchief. "What's your dog called?"

"Ben."

"Come here, Bennie – good dog, come on then, Bennie."
She began to play on the hearth-rug with him. Joyce went
to her desk to sort some bills. After a few minutes she said
"Ben, not Bennie."

114

"He likes being called Bennie, don't you, Bennie?"

"I expect your aunt will be wondering where you are," said Joyce firmly.

During the next few days Tracy drifted more and more frequently into the main part of the house. Joyce and Nora would become aware suddenly of her presence, swinging on the handle of a door, squatted on the stairs, staring. Or her voice would make them jump. "Excuse me, Miss Knight, can I ask you something? Why's that clock say the wrong time?" And, thus insinuated into the room with them, she would chatter on. My mum this, my dad that, the teacher in our school says this, when I'm at home I do that. Excuse me, Miss Knight, did you know your cardy has a button missing? Bennie likes me, doesn't he, Bennie likes me coming to see him. Did you see Eric and Ernie on telly last knight, wasn't it funny when they dressed up like Arabs, I *love* Eric and Ernie, I really love them. Do you like Eric and Ernie? Excuse me, Miss Knight, shall I open that bottle for you, my mum always puts the lid under hot water, then they shift.

"You don't need to say excuse me all the time, Tracy."

And the child, silent for a while, would stare with that look of assessment so that after a bit Nora or Joyce would start to feel uncomfortable; she had a knack of putting one at a disadvantage. There was a wizened maturity about her, a precocious worldliness; a most unchildlike child, the Misses Knight agreed, who had never had much to do with children in any case. Oh, they were fond of children, of course, smiled indulgently in the presence of the offspring of friends or neighbours. The local Cubs were allowed to clean the ground floor windows of Cader Idris in Bob-a-Job week, cheerful robust little boys who said thank you nicely for their money, looking politely upwards at you. Tracy looked upwards too – she was rather small for her age – but gave this disconcerting impression of somehow looking also downwards. And her conversation flew off at alarming tangents, you never knew where it might lead next. One day there was an embarrassing account of some feminine complaint of her mother's, full of oblique references – her you-know-where, her down-below.

"Yes," said Joyce briskly. "Now I wonder if Sylvia would like you to help her with sweeping up the leaves outside."

"Shall I take Bennie in the garden?"

The dog lay on his side, deeply asleep, occasionally twitching. His penis jutted pinkly from the long soft fur of his belly. Tracy said with interest, "He's got his thing out, for making puppies with."

Nora and Joyce had always felt that that was where a bitch was nicer. Of course, there were other problems with a bitch, but not this visible indecency. Ben was a bother; he did it a lot. "I think Ben would be better in the garden for a bit, dear." they would say to each other. Ben, shut out, would sit resentfully on the terrace, his member shrinking against the cold stone.

"Do you see, Miss Knight? Why's he doing that?"

Joyce got up jerkily, slopping the tea-cup in her hand, and opened the french window. I am going to have to have a word with Beryl, she thought, the child is supposed to stay through in their part. She watched Tracy and Ben run across the lawn together towards Sylvia, who was methodically raking leaves into golden pyramids. Beyond the lilac walk, a bonfire smoked. From the street came the sound of a loudspeaker or something, a tiresome blaring voice. And on the skyline, just above the crimson flare of the garden sumach, was the arm of some enormous crane with a pulley and a man in a glass box; how long had that been there? Joyce could not remember noticing it before. There was a sense of things pressing in, of intrusion; she closed the window again and poured another cup of tea.

It was early evening when Beryl came through to the drawing-room. She was wearing going-out clothes and spoke with some embarrassment. The thing was, she and Sylvia had promised themselves a film with a friend in Birmingham tonight, and they'd reckoned with taking Tracy along, but when it came to the point Tracy didn't want to come – there was something she fancied specially on the telly, and no getting her to budge. So would it be all right if . . . I mean, she'll put herself to bed, and she'll be happy as larry till then with her supper on a tray and the TV to watch, it's just for her to know she's not on her own in the house.

Joyce and Nora exchanged looks. It was the moment, of course, for a firm but tactful word about the Tracy situation in general. But just as Joyce (like Beryl, the dominant partner and customary spokeswoman) was starting to say, "Well, yes, Beryl, of course just for this once we . . ." the doorbell rang, Ben flew off with a fusillade of shrill barks, and Beryl was saying, "I'll get it, and thanks very much, Miss Knight, I'll tell her to be sure and not bother you."

They heard Beryl and Sylvia leave in the mini soon after seven. Their own supper, cold except for the soup to warm up in the kitchen, had been set out on the sideboard. Joyce, attending to the soup, heard the television on in the adjoining room – quickfire conversation punctuated with outbursts of laughter that swelled and receded like waves pounding a beach. She considered checking that the child was all right, rejected the idea (with a twinge of guilt) and carried the soup back to the dining-room.

They were in the drawing-room, Joyce playing patience and Nora knitting, when all the lights went out. One moment all was tranquil normality; the next they sat in isolation and confusion. "There must be a fuse gone," said Joyce. They began to tell one another to be careful, to go slowly, to try to think where the torch was. Neither of them remembered Tracy. When, a couple of minutes later, they heard the door open, Nora screamed.

Tracy said, "Bang in the middle of 'The Good Life'. Wouldn't you just know it! Pity you haven't got an open fire, Miss Knight, at my friend's they've got this real fire and when the lights went out we all sat round and did part singing, lovely it was." She seemed to be skipping round the room; her voice came now from here, now from there – Ariel-like, it chattered at them from invisibility. "Oh, do be careful, dear," cried Nora. "The little table with the Sèvres dish . . ." There was a bump and a clatter, but it was Joyce, trying to find her way to the door and stumbling against the sofa. She stood still, the familiar rendered treacherous, stranded in the middle of her own drawing-room. Tracy, her voice dodging now over to the window said, "Whoops! Can't you see where you are, Miss Knight? Here, shall I hang onto you?", and Joyce felt a moth-like brushing against her sleeve, and then a cold little hand on hers. She twitched. "Can't you feel where you are? *I* can – look, the door's over there, mind the desk, isn't it fun!" "The fuses," Nora began "Aren't they in the kitchen drawer, Joyce? Oh dear, I never know how you fit them in, they . . ." But Tracy broke in scornfully, "It's not a *fuse*, it's a power-cut, they said on the news, West Midlands and parts of the South-East, because of the strike, up to three hours, we'll have to go to bed with candles, where do you keep the candles, Miss Knight?" "Strike?" said Joyce, "Power-cut? But it's disgraceful, they haven't got any right to . . ." "Because of their money, what they earn, they want something per cent and the government says they can't. Ooh, here's Bennie – I nearly stepped on you, didn't I, Bennie?" "Three hours, but how are we expected to . . .", and now Joyce barked her shin, excruciatingly, against the fender. "Oh," cried Nora. "Are you all right, dear?", and to and fro, in the darkness, went their exclamations of annoyance and distress. The house and its contents crouched around them, turned nasty, waiting to trip or obstruct.

The phone rang, in the hall. Joyce, marooned still somewhere west of the sofa, said, "Oh, bother it, now of all times", but already Tracy's voice, receding beyond the door, was crying "I'll get it, don't worry, Miss Knight, I know where it is."

"Hello?" they heard her say, and then, "Oh, Auntie Beryl – guess what, we're having a power cut, bang in the middle of 'The Good Life'. What? Ooh, goodness, did it really? Yes. Yes, I'll tell them, auntie. No, quite all right. Yes. Not to worry, auntie – will do. 'Bye for now." And back she came, flitting confident across the rooms, her voice important with information and bad news. A breakdown. The gasket. Garages just don't want to know. Stop over the night with Mandy in Solihull and an early bus tomorrow. Terribly sorry. Put meself to bed and not be a nuisance. Candles in the landing cupboard. Ever so sorry.

Nora, too, now was on her feet. "No, I can manage, dear. Really, isn't it the limit! First the lights and now this. Surely they . . . Oh, well, we must just make the best of it. I'll find the candles" – and to Tracy, firmly – "No, Tracy, thank you very much, there are some rather fragile things in the landing cupboard and I know whereabouts the candles will be." She began to grope her way through the door and across the hall: a bump, an exclamation, a yelp. "Oh, *Ben*, get out of the way . . ." "Do be careful, Nora". "I'm all right now, I've found the bannister." Clump and shuffle up the stairs; creak of boards; another exclamation, distant now; bangs and clatters. "Here we are! I've got them, Joyce."

Steps on the stairs again, less cautious now, and . . . An awful, slithering crash. Silence. "Oh, Miss Knight, I think she's fallen down the stairs."

It seemed hours. The fumble for matches, grope for scattered candles, why doesn't she *say* anything? Tracy vanishing and then suddenly re-appearing with a blessed, reassuring beam of light – the torch, however did she find it? Never mind. And thank heavens Nora is trying now to heave herself up, groaning something about her back, saying she feels a bit queasy, don't worry, dear, be fine in a minute.

And collapses again.

It was Tracy, in the end, who dialled 999. "Excuse me, Miss Knight, you're putting your finger in the wrong hole. I can see, shall I . . ." And appeared from the kitchen, breathless and important, with cups of tea. "My mum's got this friend who's a nurse and she says it's the best thing, when you've had a shock, it steadies people up. I put two sugars in, is that O.K.?" And let the ambulancemen in and skipped from one leg to another in the now candle-lit hall, a-twitter with interest and involvement.

The reviving sight of uniformed men (on one's own side, there to serve, like policemen and commissionaires), or possibly the tea, put heart into Joyce once more. She was able to adjust her tone of voice, step aside from those awful dithery moments when even Tracy had seemed a support, and behave normally. She told Tracy to shut Ben up in the cloakroom, and exhorted the ambulancemen, shouting slightly, as though the power cut affected hearing as well as vision. "O.K. love, take it easy," they said, shooting powerful beams of torchlight into the gloom. "She's conscious, is she? Don't worry, it doesn't look like a bad one, you sit back and leave it to us now." And Joyce, explaining that she was not worried, not unduly, found herself pushed to the fringe of things, screened from Nora by large competent backs, not quite picking up what was said.

They did not think there was anything broken. Concussion, probably, X-rays. Observation. And now there was Nora being carted off, her hair all anyhow, looking white but stoical, strapped up in a nasty red blanket that somehow suppressed personality: she might have been anyone. "Right," said the ambulanceman. "We'll get off then. That's it, you come along too, that's the best thing" – as Joyce groped for her hat and coat.

Again, she forgot Tracy. It was not until she was climbing into the ambulance that she found the child at her side, bright-eyed, tucking herself into an unoccupied corner. "Oh," Joyce began, "I don't really think . . ." But they were off now, rounding the corner into the High Street, and the men were laughing at some remark of Tracy's that Joyce did not catch. "She's a card, your grand-daughter," said one of them. Joyce opened her mouth to deny relationship, but Tracy was already off on a saga of explanation. Nora turned her head to one side and closed her eyes.

Joyce and Nora, all their lives, had enjoyed good health. The occasional tiresomeness had been attended to by their G.P. – as private patients, naturally. Joyce had seldom set foot inside a hospital, except once to have a nasty boil lanced and otherwise only to visit less fortunate friends (and then with some reluctance – there but for the grace of God, and one did not want to be reminded of that). Now, she was disconcerted by the detachment and dexterity of the nurses who whisked Nora away from her down gleaming corridors. Nobody consulted her or asked her what she would like done. She sat disconsolate in a waiting-room; Tracy, beside her, was immersed in some cheap women's magazine, stuffed with advertisements for sanitary towels and deodorant. There were other people also waiting, an elderly

121

man who shuffled and muttered (possibly drunk, Joyce realised with alarm), a black woman with a small child, an adolescent boy with a radio that emitted vulgar music, turned low but still irritating. Joyce would have told him to turn it off were it not that she herself felt so uneasy in this place as to be quite without the protective armoury of personality. She felt a fish out of water, as though she were abroad (she and Nora had never cared much for abroad), as though she were displaced in time. And yet it was here and now, and she was not half a mile from St. Joseph's Place. When at last a young doctor appeared, saying, "Miss Knight?", she gathered herself with an effort and began, "Ah, now perhaps you will be so good as to take me to my sister, we must discuss various things and . . ." But the man was already explaining that the X-rays showed a cracked rib, nothing worse, though there was certainly concussion, and Nora was drowsy now, and quite comfortable in Ward C in the main building and would be best left to herself tonight, visiting hours tomorrow were from . . . "Ward?" said Joyce. "Oh no, we shall want a private room, there's been some mistake I'm afraid, my sister and I always . . ." The private wing, the doctor explained, courteous but positive, was full and no amenity beds available tonight. "Oh, but really," cried Joyce. "That won't do. Surely there must be some way of arranging something, Doctor er . . ." "Tomkins," chirped Tracy. "Doctor Kevin Tomkins. Isn't that funny, my dad's called Kevin, too!" And now Joyce saw the little white-lettered metal strip against the doctor's jacket. "Doctor Tomkins," she continued, "I'm afraid I really can't have my sister in . . ." But the young man was beaming at Tracy, saying really, fancy that now, well, well, and what's your name? And the wretched child was off on yet another spiel of my mum this, my auntie that, actually I don't live at, our house is . . . And the man also came from

Derbyshire, it appeared, which accounted for the eery similarity between his speech and Tracy's accent – a diction which, Joyce now realised, had jarred her ear for many days. She felt in even further alienation, tumbled against her will into a discordant and wayward world. It was as though the television could not be switched off, or the front door of number seven St. Joseph's Place would not close.

"Don't worry," said the doctor kindly. "Your sister will be well taken care of, I promise you. Why don't you get along home now, it's getting late." He patted Tracy on the head. "You see your auntie gets herself a nice hot drink and a good night's sleep, eh?" And Tracy, smirking, was saying, "yes 'course I will, actually it's Auntie Beryl's my auntie not . . ." at the same moment as Joyce snapped, "The little girl is not my niece. Thank you very much, doctor, no doubt I shall see you in the morning."

They took a taxi home. The power cut was over; the house blazed with light. Joyce, a little restored as she stepped into the hall, was filled with sudden rage against these unknown people, whose activities had caused the whole thing, but for whom she would be filling Nora's hot water bottle, while Nora put Ben to bed in the downstairs cloakroom. What had they to do with her, what right had they to intrude in her life? She hung up her coat with clumsy, jerky movements, while Tracy and Ben skittered about her in joyful reunion. "Oops!" said Tracy. "You've knocked down Miss Knight's hat, Miss Knight – here, I'll get it. Isn't it muddling, you both being called Miss Knight, if I was going to be here a long time I'd have to call you Auntie Joyce, wouldn't I?" She followed Joyce through into the drawing-room, singing to herself. A cheerful little soul, Beryl had said, quiet, I promise you she won't be any bother, you'll hardly know she's here.

It was half past eleven. "Time to go to bed," said Joyce

firmly. She felt more in control now, braced by the security of the house, the controlled and ordained atmosphere, nothing unchosen, nothing out of place. "Bed, Tracy. I'll just come through with you and see everything's all right."

She did not often go into the staff quarters beyond the kitchen; staff, she and Nora had always affirmed, had a right to privacy too. Now, walking into the sitting-room without knocking, she felt a little awkward. Tracy bounced ahead through the door of the small boxroom that had been turned into a bedroom and then out again, saying, "Left my nightie in their room – just have to get it." She opened the door of the other bedroom, and Joyce saw, to her surprise, a double bed. She stood staring; on a bedside table was a photograph of Beryl and Sylvia, arm in arm, in bathing costumes. Joyce said, "Oh dear, Beryl's had to turn out of her room for you."

Tracy was rummaging under the bed. She popped out, a garment in her hand. "Oh no, this is where Auntie Beryl and Auntie Sylvia sleep, in the big bed – always – they had it put in special when they came, didn't you know?" "When they . . . ?" said Joyce faintly, looking round the room now, untidy, the dressing-table a muddle of pots and bottles, a smell of powder and scent. "Didn't you know? Because of being married to each other, like ladies and men are. My mum told me, she said I'm quite old enough to know about that sort of thing and it's nothing to make a fuss about, quite a lot of people are like that, you get men marrying each other too." She giggled. "Catch me marrying another girl when I'm grown-up, I don't see the point, my mum says she wouldn't fancy it either but it's not her business and it takes all sorts to make a world. I like Auntie Sylvia, she's ever so nice – she made drop scones with me yesterday. I'll just go and clean my teeth."

Joyce stood in the doorway, looking at the bed. From the

124

bathroom came brisk sounds of scrubbing and spitting. She felt physically unsteady. It was as though the house had been shaken up around her, like the glass in a kaleidoscope, and reassembled in an unrecognizable pattern. The place had been violated – by unknown men in some power station, by the association of these women. One had always known the world was not entirely to one's own taste, and had made one's arrangements accordingly. What the eye doesn't see, the heart doesn't grieve over. It was possible, she had thought, to detach oneself, to be selective, to be in the world but not of it; tonight, a spiteful world had disputed this. She was sixty-eight, not as fit as she used to be; if this kind of thing was going to go on, she did not know for how long she could hold out.

Tracy came out of the bathroom, wearing a flowered nightdress; thin, unchildish, and as powerful as a coiled spring. She said, "Nightie-night", and then coyly, "Auntie Joyce."

Joyce went through into the main part of the house. In the hall sat Ben, wagging his tail. As he jumped at her in greeting she saw that he was protruding again beneath. Bitches they had usually had spayed. She and Nora had long ago agreed that Ben was not a complete success, but once you own an animal you are committed to it, there is nothing you can do. She shut him in the cloakroom and went upstairs to bed, slowly, the sound of the High Street traffic suddenly loud beyond the landing window.

The emasculation of Ted Roper

JEANIE BANKS, RIGID with emotion, her cardigan on inside out, muttering rehearsed words, deaf and blind to the bright morning, made her way down the village street. Past the post office, the one, two, three, four cottages, past the pub, Mrs Halliday's, the garage, the one, two, three new bungalows, the Lathams', Cardwell's yard. She stopped outside Roper's, simmering, reached out to open the gate, lost her nerve, plunged on down to the lamp-post where the village ended, yanked up her resolution again, turned, aimed back, fumbled furious with the latch on Roper's gate.

The front garden a disgrace, as always, strewn with empty oil cans, plastic sacks, rusting iron objects, the excretions of Roper's hand-to-mouth odd-jobbing dealing-in-this-and-that existence. Furtive, unreliable, transacting in dirty pound notes, dodging his taxes without a doubt, down the pub every evening. Dirty beggar, cocky as a robin, sixty if he was a day.

Feeling swelled to a crescendo, and courage with it; she hammered on the door. Then again. And again. No answer. He'd be there all right, he'd be there, nine-thirty in the morning, since when did Roper go out and do a decent day's work? She shoved at the side gate.

He was round the back, fiddling about with a great pile of

timber, good timber at that, planks all sizes and shapes and how did he come by it one would like to know? A whole lot of tyres stacked up in one corner, stuff spilling out of the shed, filth everywhere.

"Hello, Jeanie."

She halted, breathless now. Words fail you, they do really. They leave you huffing and puffing, at a disadvantage, seeing suddenly the run in your tights, seeing yourself reflected in the eyes of others – angry, dumpy, middle-aged widow, just Jeanie Banks. In the beady spicy nasty eyes of Ted Roper, stood there in the middle of his junk like a little farmyard cock. A randy strutting bantam cock.

"What can I do for you, Jeanie?"

She said, "It's not what you can do it's what's been done, that's what's the trouble."

"Trouble?" He took out tobacco, a grubby roll of cigarette papers. "Trouble?" His dirty fingers rolling, tapping, his tongue flickering over the paper.

"My Elsa's expecting."

"Expecting?" he said. "Oh – expecting." A thin smile now, a thin complacent smile. Grinning away at it, the old bastard, pleased as punch. As if it were something to be proud of, as if it did him credit even, stood there with his thumbs stuck in his trouser pockets like those boys in western films. Some boy – Ted Roper. Boy my foot, sixty if he's anything.

"That's what I said. Expecting."

He put the cigarette in his mouth; thin smoke fumed into the village sunshine. Not trousers, she saw now. Jeans – jeans just like young men wear, slumped down on his thin hips, the zip sliding a bit, a fullness you couldn't miss below, stuck out too the way he stood, legs apart, thumbs in pockets.

THE EMASCULATION OF TED ROPER

"Well," he said, "I s'pose that'd be in the nature of things. She's getting a big girl now."

Grinning away there, wiry and perky and as blatant as you like. She felt her outrage surge.

"It's rape," she said. "That's what it damn well is. A little creature like that, a little young thing. Bloody rape!" The colour rushed to her cheeks; she didn't use language like that, not she, never.

"Now, now, Jeanie. Who's to know who gave who the come on."

She exploded. She shouted, "You take that blasted cat to the vet, Ted Roper, and get it seen to, the rest of us have just about had enough, there's kittens from one end of the village to the other and my Elsa was nothing but a kitten herself." She swung round and stormed to the gate. When she looked back he was still standing there, the cigarette laid on his lower lip, his jeans fraying at the crotch, the grin still on his face. "Or you'll find it done for you one of these days!"

All the way back to the cottage her heart thumped. It didn't do you any good, getting yourself into a state like that, it took it out of you, she'd be jumpy all day now. Back home in the kitchen, she made herself a cup of tea. The old cat, the mother, was sprawled in the patch of sun on the mat and Elsa was in the armchair. When Jeanie came in she jumped down and shimmied across the floor: pretty, grace-ful, kittenish and distinctly lumpy, no doubt about it, that unmistakeable pear-shape forming at the end of her. And Jeanie, subsiding into the chair, drinking her tea, eyed her and eyed the old cat, not so old come to that, five or was it six, and as she did so a whole further implication leaped into the mind – why hadn't she thought of it before, how dis-gusting, if it were people you could have them slapped in prison for that.

"Fact is," said her sister Pauline, that afternoon, "there's probably hardly a one in the village isn't his. Being the only tom round about, bar him on Lay's farm and he's beyond it if you ask me. So you let Ted Roper have it? Good on you, Jeanie."

Jeanie, cooler now, calmer, righteous and ever so slightly heroic, went over it all again, word for word: I said, he said, so I said, and him as cocky as you like.

"He's a cocky little so-and-so," said Pauline. "Always was. I bet he got the wind up a bit though, Jeanie, with you bawling him out, you're bigger than he is." She chuckled. "Hey – d'you remember the time they got him in the girls' playground and Marge ripped the belt off his trousers so he had to hold 'em up all afternoon? God – laugh . . . ! Donkeys' years ago . . ."

"Funny, isn't it," Pauline went on, "there's four of us in the village still as were at school with Ted. You, me, Nellie Baker, Marge. Randy he was, too. Remember?"

"Funny he's never married," said Jeanie.

Pauline snorted. "Out for what he can get, that one. Not that he'd get it that often, is my guess."

"Can't stand the man. Never could. 'Nother cup? Anyway, what I say is, he ought to be made to have something done about that cat. It's shocking. Shocking."

In the basket chair the old cat raucously purred; Elsa, in a patch of sunlight, lay flirting with a length of string.

"Sick of drowning kittens, I am," said Jeanie. "I'll have to get her seen to after, like I did the old cat. Shame."

"Shame."

The two women contemplated the cats.

"I mean, we wouldn't care for it, if it were you or me."

"Too right."

"Not," said Pauline, "at that time of life. That's a young creature, that is, she's got a right to, well, a right to things."

"Hysterectomy's the nearest, if it were a person."

"That's it, Jeanie. And you'd not hear of that if it were a girl. Another matter if it's in middle life."

"That cat of Roper's," said Jeanie, "must be going on twelve or thirteen."

Later, as she walked to the shop, Roper's pick-up passed her, loaded with slabs of timber, belting too fast down the village street, Roper at the wheel, one arm on the sill, a young lad beside him, one of the several who hung around him. She saw Roper see her, turn to the boy, say something, the two of them roar grinning across the cross-roads. She stood still, seething.

"Cardwell's boy, weren't that?" said Marge Tranter, stopping also. "With Roper."

"I daresay. What they see in that old devil . . ."

"Men's talk. Dirty stories, that stuff. Norman says he doesn't half go on in the pub, Roper. He's not a one for that kind of thing, Norman isn't. He says Roper holds out hours on end sometimes, sat there in the corner with his mates. Showing off, you know."

"Fat lot he's got to show off about," said Jeanie. "A little runt, he is. Always was. I was saying to Pauline, remember the time you . . ."

"Pulled his trousers down, wasn't it? Don't remind me of that, Jeanie, I'll die . . ."

"Not pulled them down, it wasn't. Took his belt. Anyway, Marge, I gave him an earful this morning, I'll tell you that. That cat of his has been at my Elsa. I went straight down there and I said look here Ted Roper . . ."

A quarter of a mile away Ted Roper's pick-up, timber dancing in the back, dodged in and out of the traffic on the A34, overtaking at sixty, cutting in, proving itself. Cardwell's boy and Roper, blank-faced, be-jeaned, the cowboys of the shires, rode the Oxfordshire landscape.

In the village and beyond, Roper's cat – thin, rangy, one-eyed and fray-eared – went about his business.

And, according to the scheme of things, the ripe apples dropped from the trees, the *jeunesse dorée* of the area switched their allegiance from the Unicorn to the Hand and Shears taking with them the chattering din of un-muffled exhausts and the reek of high-octane fuel, the road flooded at the railway bridge and Jeanie's Elsa swelled soft and sagging like the bag of a vacuum cleaner.

"Several at least," said Jeanie. "Half a dozen, if you ask me. Poor little thing, it's diabolical."

"There's a side to men," said Pauline, "that's to my mind just not like us and that's the only way you can put it. And I don't mean sex, nothing wrong with that when the time and the place are right. I mean . . ."

"It's a kind of men rather, I'd say. Harry's not that way, nor was my Jim. I mean, there's men that are normal men in the proper way but don't go on about it."

"In Italy," said Pauline, "all the men are the other kind. All of them. From the word go. Young boys and all. They wear bathing costumes cut deliberately so you can see everything they've got."

"Which is something you can take as read, in a normal man. It doesn't need shouting about."

"Exactly. If I were you, Jeanie, I'd give that cat a drop of cod liver oil in her milk. She's going to need all her strength."

Perhaps also according to the scheme of things, Ted Roper's pick-up, a while later, was involved in circumstances never clarified in a crash with Nellie Baker's Escort at the village cross-roads. No blood was shed and the pick-up, already so battle-scarred as to be impervious, lived to fight again, but the Escort was crippled and Nellie Baker too shaken and confused to be able to sort out exactly what had happened except for a strong conviction that aggression had been involved. At the Womens' Institute committee meeting she held forth.

"He came out of nowhere and was into me before I knew what was happening. I was either stopped or the next best thing, that I'll swear."

"What does he say?"

"Whatever he's saying's being said to the police. He took off, without a word hardly. It was Mr Latham ran me home and got the garage for me. I've told them my side of it, at the police station. It's up to them now."

"The police," said Jeanie Banks, "have been down at Ted Roper's more than once. Asking about this and that. They could do some asking just now, the stuff he's got there and one wonders where it all comes from."

"The police," said Pauline, "are men. Remember Ted Roper at school, Nellie? Jeanie and I were talking about that only the other day – how we used to take him down a peg or two."

And, according to a scheme of things or not, no case was brought against Ted Roper for careless driving or dangerous driving or aggression or anything at all. Those who failed to see how that pick-up could have passed its MOT continued to speculate; Ted Roper's insurance company ignored letters from Nellie Baker's insurance company.

Jeanie's Elsa had five kittens, two of them stillborn.

Ted Roper, wiry and self-assured as his cat, continued to cruise the local roads, to make his corner of the pub an area of masculine assertion as impenetrable and complacent as the Athenaeum. From it came gusts of hoarse laughter and anecdotes which were not quite audible, bar certain key words.

It may have been the stillborn kittens that did it, as much as anything, those damp limp little rags of flesh. Or the sight of the emptied Elsa, restored to a former litheness but subtly altered, wise beyond her years. Or months.

Jeanie, tight-lipped, visited Marge to borrow her cat basket.

"You'll take her to be done, then?"

"Have to, won't I? Or it'll be the same thing over again."

"Shame."

"Just what Pauline said."

Marge, lining the cat basket with a piece of old blanket, paused. "It's like with people. Always taken for granted it must be the woman. Pills, messing about with your insides . . ." She swung the door of the basket shut and tested the catch. "There's an alternative, Jeanie. Thought of that?"

"What do you think I was down Ted Roper's for, that time?"

"And much joy you got out of it. No, what I'm thinking of is we see to it ourselves."

The two women stared at each other over the cat basket. Marge, slowly, even rather terribly, smiled. "I wouldn't mind, I wouldn't half mind, giving Ted Roper his come-uppance."

In a village, people come and go all day. Women, in particular – to and from the school, the shop, the bus stop, each other's houses. The little group of Jeanie, Pauline, Marge and Nellie Baker, moving in a leisurely but somehow intent way around the place that afternoon, glancing over garden walls and up the sides of cottages, was in no way exceptional. Nor, unless the observer were of a peculiarly enquiring turn of mind, was the fact that they carried, between them, a cat basket, a pair of thick leather gardening gloves, and a half a pound of cod wrapped in newspaper.

Presently, the cat basket now evidently heavy and bouncing a little from side to side, they emerged somewhat breathless from the field behind the pub and made their way rather hurriedly to the garage of Nellie Baker's house, where an old Morris replaced the deceased Escort. The Morris drove away in the direction of Chipping Norton passing, incidentally, the very school playground where once, donkey's years ago, four outraged and contemptuous schoolgirls had a go at the arrogance of masculine elitism.

In a village, also, change is more quickly observed than you might think. Even change so apparently insignificant as the girth of a cat. In this case, it was habits as much as girth. A cat that has previously roamed and made the night hideous, and which takes instead to roosting, eyes closed and paws folded, in the sun on the tops of walls, idling away the time, will be noticed.

And the more so when the change eerily extends to the cat's owner.

At first it was just the paunch jutting below the sagging belt of Ted Roper's jeans. Then, balancing the paunch, came a fullness to the face, a thickening of the stubbly cheeks, a definite double chin. "Put on a bit, haven't you, Ted?" people said. "Have to cut down on the beer, eh?" And Ted would wryly grin, without the perky come-back that might have been expected. With physical expansion went a curious decline of those charismatic qualities: the entourage of youths dropped off. Some nights, Ted sat alone in the pub, staring into his glass with the ruminative and comfortably washed-up look of his seniors. A series of mishaps befell the pick-up: punctures stranding Ted on remote roads, a catastrophic fuel leak, a shattered windscreen. It was driven, presently, in a more sedate way; it no longer rode or cruised but rattled and pottered.

It was as though the old assertive stringy cocky Ted were devoured and enveloped, week after week, by this flabby amiable lethargic newcomer. The jeans gave way to a pair of baggy brown cords. He began to leave his corner of the public bar and join the central group around the fireplace; there, the talk was of onions, the ills of the nation, weather and fuel prices.

And, in the village or outside his own gate, meeting Nellie Baker, say, or Marge or Pauline or Jeanie Banks, he would pass the time of day, initiate a bit of chat, offer small gifts by way of surplus timber, useful lino offcuts, the odd serviceable tyre.

"Poor old so-and-so," said Pauline. "They're easily taken down, aren't they? That's what comes of depending on the one thing. You can almost feel sorry for them."

Due 28 Days From Latest Date

SEP 2 0 1986	JUL 22 1991		
OCT 4 1986	JAN 17 1992		
OCT 8 1986			
OCT 2 2 1986	AUG 29 1994		
OCT 3 0 1986	AUG 0 9 2003		
NOV 2 5 1986			
MAY 1 6 1987	WITHDRAWN		
FEB 1 7 1989			
JUL - 2 1990			